OUTBACK HERO

Kate and her brother, Pete, had always been happy on their family's homestead in Australia, but now they are being forced to sell it; after their mother was killed in a plane crash, their father had drunk himself to death, leaving them heavily in debt. Their neighbour, Mark Thornton, wishes to buy the property, but Kate deeply resents him because he had been the pilot of the plane in which their mother died. But, finally, Kate is forced to confront her real feelings about Mark . . .

Books by Noelene Jenkinson
in the Linford Romance Library:

A WHIRLWIND ROMANCE

NOELENE JENKINSON

OUTBACK HERO

Complete and Unabridged

LINFORD
Leicester

First published in Great Britain in 2000

First Linford Edition
published 2003

British Library CIP Data

Jenkinson, Noelene
    Outback hero.—Large print ed.—
Linford romance library
1. Love stories
2. Large type books
I. Title
823.9'14 [F]

ISBN 1–8439–5035–9

Published by
F. A. Thorpe (Publishing)
Anstey, Leicestershire

Set by Words & Graphics Ltd.
Anstey, Leicestershire
Printed and bound in Great Britain by
T. J. International Ltd., Padstow, Cornwall

This book is printed on acid-free paper

1

Through the wire screen door, Kate Reed's eyes narrowed and her mouth pulled into a thin line. The silver Range Rover glinted in the hot, morning sun as she watched it approach along the gum-tree-lined driveway to the homestead. A surge of resentment rolled through her. This visitor to her beloved debt-ridden Darnleigh was no stranger. She'd known Mark Thornton all her life.

The chunky vehicle tyres crunched to a stop on the gravel before the two-storey red brick house. A cloud of following dust lingered in the air before settling again to the dry brown earth. Her neighbour uncurled his long, muscular frame from the vehicle and slammed the door.

Kate had amassed a resentful dam of memories over the past six years. It was unfair, she knew, all the more difficult to maintain with the best-looking hunk of manhood in the district limping across her driveway in the Australian heat. Seeing Mark again at her father's funeral the week before, Kate had been appalled to discover that her heart still turned over at the sight of him. But what woman wouldn't succumb to his rugged good looks, easy manner and deep, sexy drawl?

She had also been shocked to notice that he walked with a bracing stiffness on his left side. In typical Thornton style, he carried his minor handicap with poise. Idly, she wondered if his leg ever hurt, then cursed her weakness in feeling the smallest grain of sympathy for him. He looked so strong, so dynamic, so alive. She felt bitter-sweet heartache wash through her. The tall, commanding man hadn't lost any of his appeal, which only highlighted the unbelievable reality that the most eligible bachelor in the district remained unmarried.

The past five days had proved an apprehensive ordeal waiting to see if or when he would visit. Ironically, now that he was here, her big brother, Pete, was away from the homestead repairing boundary fences, getting the property ready for sale. Confronted with Mark alone, she could have used the extra strength of Pete's moral support.

Kate was flooded with painful regret. If her inept, stubborn father hadn't mismanaged their property, she and Pete wouldn't be forced to sell, Darnleigh wouldn't be up for grabs, and Mark Thornton wouldn't have offered to buy it. Filled with the impossible hope of reclaiming her happy childhood and restoring the remnants of her once-whole family before it had been cruelly shattered by fate, Kate rubbed her arms and scowled.

In that instant, Mark's head jerked up. Beneath a battered, wide-brimmed hat which shaded his face, eyes as rich and brown as the thousands of acres of soil he owned met and captured her own unsmiling stare. Deep lines edged their outer corners and a sparkle of warm familiarity lit them from within. Kate's heart set up an alarming pounding. One glance revived the knowledge that he was a strong, magnetic personality with whom to remain guarded. Fortunately, the harder side of his personality was tempered by a persuasive mischief lurking just beneath the surface.

Not bothering to use the wide, stone steps, and using his good right leg for propulsion, Mark's stiff leap brought him on to the generous veranda that surrounded the old house. Kate sucked in a steadying breath of apprehension and awe. She forced herself into neighbourly action, ungraciously thrusting open the paint-flaked door. She winced at the sound, one of many that exposed the property's run-down condition.

'Welcome home, Katie.'

How well she remembered that deep,

rich voice which rumbled so smoothly and effortlessly from his chest like thick syrup as he had used the fond nickname he'd gifted her when they were kids. Determined not to be emotionally undone at his expense ever again, and bracing herself for the forthcoming encounter, she stiffened.

'Katelyn,' she said.

'What happened to Katie?' he asked pensively.

'She grew up.'

Her irritation at his playful familiarity turned to outright surprise when he caught her hands in his. Their big brown warmth covered her own slender fingers, and his thumbs stroked her pulsating wrists. When he suddenly leaned forward, Kate realised he intended to kiss her. Not wanting to test her resistance, knowing she would fail, she turned her face aside and his warm, full lips brushed her cheek softly instead. The feel of his mouth on her skin sent a flash of excitement through her and she despised herself for enjoying the featherlight sensation.

When they broke apart again and Kate hastily removed her hands, clenching them at her side, a flash of puzzlement at her rejection crossed his face.

'Nice to have you back.'

'Is it?'

'Always.'

'Not for long,' she answered, especially if she was successful in getting the European promotion — she expected a telephone call any day now. 'Pete isn't here,' she added.

'I didn't come to see your brother. I came to see you.'

His piercing gaze travelled over her as he removed his hat, exposing a familiar crop of thick brown sun-streaked hair. His dark eyes took in her sleeveless blue top and brief white shorts above a pair of trim legs. She prickled with hot awareness, marginally gratified by the scrutiny but considering his lengthy stare more than neighbourly.

'Forgotten what I look like?' Kate

quipped, uncomfortable.

'Never.'

The word emerged almost as a threat. The back of one large hand swiped his damp forehead and he slapped the dust from his hat against a muscled thigh, tight in faded denims.

'Get me a cold drink before I evaporate in this heat.'

'Still as bossy as ever. You don't own Darnleigh. Yet,' she tossed at him over her shoulder and let the door slam in his face.

Waiting for a strong retort that never came, Kate walked stiff-backed down the hall and into the kitchen.

'I've made the best offer you'll get, Katie.'

Mark's voice echoed softly, close behind. Despite his slight handicap, he had moved fast. She clenched her teeth at the nickname again, but the coldness of the flagged stone floor beneath her bare feet soothed her jangled nerves as she crossed to the refrigerator and poured them an icy drink. She deliberately set his frosted glass on the table, sipping her own and eyeing him with a challenging gleam. She had no intention of playing the friendly hostess when she didn't feel it.

He grinned and tossed his hat on to the table as though throwing it into the ring, retrieved his drink and sculled the contents in one draught, leaving his mouth glistening with dewy moisture. Kate privately drooled over the marked and impressed change in him. Like a prestigious vintage wine, Mark Thornton had improved with age. He'd always possessed that air of authority and control. Combined with an increased and devastating physical appeal, he bordered on dangerous. Remembering him when she was a besotted, naïve sixteen-year-old, his towering height and powerful build had promised then what time had generously delivered — a magnificent specimen of manhood.

'Don't think that just because you have me alone without Pete, you can talk me around,' she warned.

'A man would have more than talk on his mind around you,' he drawled.

Kate was infuriated to notice a twinkle in his eyes and an angry flush raced across her face. The flirt! He was using a big come-on. What a cheek.

'OK, I'm suitably flattered. But you can cut out the nonsense,' she suggested with saccharin sweetness, 'and get down to business.'

He pulled out a chair, turned it around and sat on it backwards. Folding his arms across the back of it, he said, 'I'm sorry about what's happened to this place, Katie.'

If he called her that one more time . . .

'Yeah, right! I'll believe that when hell freezes over. You can't wait to get your hands on it.'

His dark brows cinched into a frown and his forehead wrinkled as if he was genuinely puzzled.

'Not true.'

'What is then?'

'That I care about you and Pete, and your future,' he replied smoothly.

Kate faltered at his quiet words, outwardly at least filled with what appeared to be genuine sincerity and warmth.

'Is that what your offer's about? Charity? Because if it is, Pete and I don't want it. We'll manage just fine.'

'Katie, I can understand your anger.'

'I'm more than angry. I despise my weak, drunken father for driving us to this and letting Pete's inheritance slip through his incompetent fingers.'

'Your father wasn't all to blame. He never fully recovered after the war.'

His subtle insinuation referred to the state of her father's mental health but he was being tactful.

'Your father returned to live a normal life,' she replied.

Mark shrugged.

'On the surface maybe but he had his bad moments, too. The war affected some men more than others. Most coped. Some didn't. None of them forgot.'

'Life might have been easier around this place if he had.'

'What about your share of Darnleigh?'

Kate's contempt for her father, even in death, laced her voice.

'What's left of it. I'll manage. I'm not concerned about myself but I'm worried about Pete. He needs my half to help him in buying another property, a much smaller one,' she added with bitterness. 'He shouldn't have to do that, lower his dreams, I mean, and start at the bottom. He'll probably have to move away from this district where he was born and grew up, leave all his friends. He should have been able to take over and carry on here, build on what already exists. I know he could make a go of this place. Farming's in his blood.'

Kate hated the look of pity that crossed Mark's face. To stop him uttering another soothing platitude and to feed his thoughts, she doled out a little further juicy information to tantalise every competitive bone in his body.

'I hope you don't think you're the only player in this game.'

That diverted him. His clear gaze hardened.

'Someone else wants to buy Darnleigh?'

'You're not the only big shot in the district with money. We might be down to our subsoil in debt but, handled properly, this place is still a viable proposition.'

'I'm well aware of that,' he responded calmly, 'otherwise I wouldn't be interested.'

Grinning, she tilted her head to one side.

'Afraid of a little competition?'

He sent her a cool, steady gaze.

'I doubt it. Who is it?'

Kate found his composure unsettling but she'd bet every last acre of Darnleigh she could ruffle that smooth exterior when she told him who it was. He wasn't going to like it but Pete's future was at stake.

'Jack Donohue.'

Mark hissed out a long, slow blast of breath, his gaze incredulous.

'You'd deal with that crook? Six years of city life and smog have dulled your wits, Katie. You used to be smart.'

She felt a twinge of hurt whip through her.

'He's made a genuine offer, just like you.'

'Donohue? Genuine?' Mark scoffed. 'And did this upright paragon of virtue happen to mention exactly what he'd do with the property if he bought it?'

Kate hesitated. Many doubts filled her life at the moment and any buyer, especially if unscrupulous, only added to them. But Donohue was another prospect and, when it came down to the bottom line, that was all that mattered. The more contenders, the higher the sale price to give Pete a healthy start out on his own. Despite her misgivings,

Kate tried to match her voice with her careless shrug.

'What's the difference, as long as we get our money?'

'That attitude's not like you, Katie. You love this place, this countryside. You wouldn't change a lifetime's opinions overnight. What's behind all this?'

Kate scooped up their glasses from the table and took them across to the sink. She looked out the kitchen window, across the distant golden wheat stubble stretching away from the house for miles. Ironically, the summer's harvest just stripped had been the best in the district for years but would still be nowhere near enough to release them from their debts. The country was in her blood. Every day she longed and vowed to return to it, somehow. It was the reason she ditched the city most weekends in her four-wheel drive, or went horse riding with friends to lose herself in the bush.

14

But career opportunities for photographic journalists didn't exist out here, and although she'd built up a small side income from exhibitions and sales of her private work, it wasn't nearly enough to support herself yet and she didn't have enough of a nest egg to go it alone and try. She'd sent every spare dollar she earned back to Pete on Darnleigh, knowing his financial struggles and problems with their father.

'Katie?' Mark growled.

She shuffled at the sink.

'I know Donohue's a property developer,' she muttered. 'He might have mentioned he'd subdivide.'

Mark exploded from his chair and paced about. Kate swung her apprehensive gaze back to watch him and listen.

'In broadacre farming country? That's outrageous. Nobody makes a living out here on smallholdings. You get big or you get out.'

He swept a suntanned arm wide,

encompassing the room.

'You'd watch him flatten this historic mansion to a pile of bricks?'

'It won't come to that,' she said but she sounded weak and ineffectual.

'The only way you can guarantee it is to sell to me.'

He advanced towards her and his arms reached out, as if to grab her but, after a moment's thought, he dropped them and clamped his hands on his hips as if in restraint.

'Katie, you know the man,' Mark said and scowled down at her. 'He promises one thing and delivers the opposite. Any contract will be in his favour, not yours. He's not known for his willing community spirit and generosity.'

'And you are? I thought you said your offer wasn't charity.'

'It's not. Farming's a tough business these days. No-one can afford to be sentimental. But you know I'll do what's best for this property. Can you say the same about Donohue?'

'Everybody knows what he's like.'

Kate tried to be casual and play down his opposition.

'But he's interested, and that's all we need.'

All along, Kate had considered the idea of selling her home absurd. Initially, Pete wanted to but she didn't. Kate wanted to fight, ride out the nightmare, take their chances over the coming seasons and, with better management, drag Darnleigh free of debt. It would take years but Kate wanted them to try. This was Pete's home and, for his sake much more than her own, Kate didn't want to let it go. She'd even pledged her continued financial support, the reason the overseas job was so important. Her salary would double and she could have helped him even more.

Kate tilted up her chin and looked Mark directly in the eye.

'Do you know what you're doing?' he was saying, chipping away at her resolve. 'You're signing a death warrant for this house and every paddock that goes with it. Does Pete agree with all this?'

'Of course. It was his idea to sell, not mine. I only agreed on the condition that we hold out for the very best price we can get. If that means considering Donohue as a prospect, then we will.'

Kate wasn't highly in favour of Donohue but for personal reasons she had yet to overcome she wasn't too thrilled about Mark's interest in Darnleigh either.

'Well, I thrive on a challenge. I'm just disappointed you didn't choose a more worthy opponent,' he muttered.

Deep down, regardless of the animosity Kate felt against him, Mark's opinion mattered to her and his judgement stung.

'His money's as good as yours.'

'It's not as clean or hard-earned and I never made a dollar at someone else's expense or happiness. Be warned, Katie. I don't fancy Donohue's desecration in my back yard. I'll outbid everyone to get this place.'

'Good. You have the money. We need it.'

Mark sighed and shook his head. He was so close, his breath whispered across her face. This time when his hands extended they rested on her bare shoulders. Jolted by her reaction to his light touch, Kate ran a nervous tongue over her lips and gasped in a ragged breath.

It was still painful recalling how her father had made all their lives a misery, how he had treated their mother like a possession and forced her to endure a difficult, loveless marriage. And as if their family life hadn't been unbearable enough, she had been tossed emotionally adrift at sixteen when a plane tragedy killed her mother, severing the only thread of warmth and love Kate had ever known. In the two dark years that followed, she had clashed mercilessly with her father. The day after she finished high school, Kate had packed and left Darnleigh for good.

Although she and Pete had kept in

touch in the intervening six years, she hadn't returned home until her father's death ten days ago, an event which, to Kate's amazement, had sharpened her burning resentment for Mark Thornton who, she still couldn't help thinking, was the catalyst for messing up her life.

'Katie?'

Mark's crisp tone broke into her thoughts.

'It's Katelyn! Stop calling me Katie!'

He frowned over her reminder.

'Why don't you really want me to buy Darnleigh?'

She longed to unload her emotional baggage but stopped herself.

'How can you ask that?' she whispered. 'Of course I don't want to sell, to you or anybody. I don't want Pete to lose his home.'

He shook his head, obviously not believing her.

'No, Katie, it's more than that. What?'

Kate clasped her hands together, whitening her knuckles, enduring the bleak desolation she felt inside. She didn't even know the reason herself why she retained this deep antagonism for him. She only knew that it had resurfaced and consumed her when she was around him again. Bad memories, heartache and loss.

It was obvious from Mark's attitude toward her and innocent questions that he had no idea she felt as she did. So far, he'd made no mention of the tragedy that had devastated their families six years ago. She wondered if it was because he felt any portion of guilt or wished to spare her feelings. One day, she promised herself, she would tell him exactly how much it had cost her and why there would probably always be a barrier against them recapturing the closeness and friendship of their youth.

Unable to endure his stare any longer, Kate cast a vacant look out of the kitchen window, past Mark's vehicle and the dry garden baking in the morning sun, across the front paddock and the winding lane of trees that followed the creek separating their two properties, to the low hills of the Back Ranges beyond. How much longer would she be able to enjoy this familiar and ruggedly-beautiful scene? With renewed determination, she forced herself to face him again.

'You have enough acreage on Grey Gums. Why on earth would you want more?'

Maybe she was being unfair but would a true friend pounce on a neighbour's misfortune as swiftly as Mark had done? Emotionally drained since her father's death, his funeral, dealing with the truth and late-night discussions with Pete to try and resolve it, Kate wasn't feeling charitable.

'Land is always a sound investment.'

Kate's lips twisted wryly.

'If it's properly managed.'

She paused, wishing the tension and distance between them would miraculously disappear and the past could be rewritten.

'Why, Mark? Why do you really want Darnleigh? You certainly don't need it. Grey Gums is the biggest property in the district.'

Kate watched him struggle with a reply.

'Besides being a potentially lucrative commercial proposition, and despite the fact that you're proud and don't want a hand-out, I am doing this to help out you and Pete.'

His gaze met and held hers for a long, hypnotic moment.

'We were all best mates.'

'Once,' Kate muttered.

'Why not now?'

Kate wanted to scream. If he kept pushing, she'd relent and tell him and ruin their friendship for ever. That consequence was too painful to contemplate. She shrugged.

'We were younger then. Life was less complicated.'

'I thought we knew each other too well for time to make a difference, Katie.'

Annoyed at her susceptibility to every look and change in his voice and eyes, she snapped, 'Katelyn!'

Instantly alert at her fierce and sudden outburst, Mark crossed the big homestead kitchen, eating up the space between them with long, slow strides. After his predatory approach, he loomed over her.

'That's another thing. Why don't you want me to call you Katie? You never used to mind.'

His brown eyes trapped her with such intensity she couldn't look anywhere else. Needing an answer Kate was reluctant to provide, but cornered into an explanation, she faltered over the first lame excuse that came to mind.

'It's a childish name.'

'It's the name I've called you all my life. The name I gave to a cute girl, who's turned into a beautiful woman.'

One of his hands lifted and gently brushed back a fall of her silky hair.

'Your hair was longer then. It streamed down your back and floated around you in the water when we swam in the creek. Remember?'

Unable to speak, she nodded. His mouth tugged into a twisted grin.

'You always seemed a summer girl. Your hair was as golden as the grains of wheat and your eyes as clear as a Wimmera sky. At least that much hasn't changed, but the rest of your attitude has.'

His gaze searched her face. Mentally and emotionally, Kate tried pulling back from him, away from his touch and the memories, and the love that conflicted with hate.

'You're tense, Kate, and wary. There's something about you that wasn't there before.'

She swallowed and skirted the truth. 'After six years, people change.'

'Is it losing this place?' he asked gently.

That one she could answer honestly. 'No.'

She folded her arms and rubbed them, feeling a cold shiver of emptiness despite the summer heat.

'There were so many family arguments, and so much unhappiness in later years. I'm afraid it holds no place in my heart any more.'

'You travelled a tough road growing up here.'

Mark's voice acquired a disarming softness. She forced a weak smile.

'Well, those days are over. Pete's a born farmer. I've always assumed and accepted that he would one day live and work this property, until now,' she added grimly.

'Then I don't understand, Kate. If it's not losing Darnleigh, what is it? What's really eating you?'

'Nothing.'

'Don't give me that. I know you.'

'You think you do. It's been six years. You wouldn't like me if you did.'

'I'll decide. Is it selling to me because I've got so much land already?'

Kate shook her head. When she lowered her gaze to inspect the floor, her hair swung down over her face. In a tender movement, Mark combed his fingers through its creamy colour and held it back, cupping her cheek with one hand and touching a finger of his other hand to her chin, lifting her eyes to meet his.

'Something I've said or done?'

She felt as if someone had punched the air out of her chest. He was so accurate, it was uncanny, and terrifying, because at this moment she both adored and despised him.

'If I tell you, you'll hate me.'

'Only if you sell to Donohue,' he said with a touch of humour. 'I'm your best choice and you know it.'

Kate knew she had to harden herself against him to get through this.

'I disagree.'

'Why not? Don't you trust me?'

It wasn't easy hurting him but if she was to overcome this prejudice, she must.

'I want to but I can't.'

'You always used to.'

'That was before — '

Kate stopped when she realised her mistake and how easily the words had slipped out. Now that the moment had come, she wanted to die rather than continue but she had stumbled beyond the point of no return with no option but to finish. Mark returned a wary look.

'Before what?'

She looked at him squarely and said, 'Before the plane crash.'

For one brief second, he didn't understand, then a horrified realisation shadowed its way across his face. Mark paled beneath his tan.

'It changed all our lives,' he replied in a husky whisper.

'I know, but I don't just hold a grudge, Mark. I hate you!'

Kate waited but it didn't come — the satisfaction she always imagined would be hers when this moment came. And what ate into her heart even more was the sick and devastated look on Mark's face, as though someone had just stolen his every reason to live.

'You can't mean it.'

Kate shook her head vigorously, determinedly blinking aside the moisture in her eyes. She felt herself trembling as she made her admission.

'I do, with every ounce of my being. I hate you because you were flying the plane that killed my mother. I'm sorry, Mark. I've tried, but I just can't forgive you.'

2

At last, the words were out. Mark knew and they would never be friends again. The thought quietly appalled Kate. Strangely, having finally uttered what she had longed to say for six years, she felt no release. Instead, shame haunted her words, and she discovered she had merely traded one private anguish for another.

Kate felt consumed by a lonely ache that she had ruined the only friendship she cared about, a regret that conflicted with family loyalty and the fact that Mark survived the plane wreckage but her mother did not. A beautiful woman killed in the prime of life — this, more than anything, was a loss she had never accepted. Kate watched Mark's entire body grow still, and a crushing hurt and desolation steal across his face. For a long time, she suffered his disbelieving stare. She had no idea of his thoughts.

For a long moment, they measured each other. Kate saw the character lines in his suntanned face that had etched deeper with the years. He was far from the young man she remembered, her perfect idol who could do no wrong. He had matured into the dynamic man before her, deeply attractive to her. Unfortunately, six years ago, he had shattered her naïve, romantic illusions and shaken her trust to its foundations. She resented him for that as much as his part in her mother's early and sudden death.

With slow deliberation, Mark turned away and leaned over the kitchen table, placing his hands squarely on its scrubbed wooden surface.

'I had no idea,' he said, with his back to her, his voice cool and quiet.

'You wanted the truth,' she whispered, her nerves jangling.

'Still waters,' he murmured.

Feeling confused and miserable, and

believing time would prove an ally, Kate suggested, 'Perhaps you should leave.'

He cast an agonised glance over his shoulder.

'We need to talk.'

'Please, Mark. Not today.'

'You owe me that much.'

'All right. But not now.'

He straightened and hesitated.

'Katie . . . '

She almost crumbled at the raw, gentle pleading in his voice, the bewildered gaze that searched her face. Impatiently, she shook her head.

'Just go, please.'

It squeezed her heart to see the devastation on his face. Six years of animosity warred against precious childhood memories and a teenage crush. Kate's heart pounded with tension. Mark cast her one final look of appeal then, to Kate's relief, scooped up his hat.

'I'll be back,' he muttered and strode from the room.

She heard his heavy footsteps down

the hall as he left, then the back door whined and slammed. Through the kitchen window, she watched him descend the front steps. At the bottom, he paused and turned. She caught his angry glare before he crammed the hat on his head and crossed the yard to his vehicle. Soon, a thinning dust cloud was the only visible sign left of Mark's return to Grey Gums.

Kate poured another cold drink to calm her nerves and sat down at the big timber table where a hunched Mark had stood moments before. Her hand shook and made the ice-cubes clink in her glass. If he had never flown his plane that day, and it had never crashed, her mother would still be alive. She would only have been fifty. Kate finished the icy liquid in large gulps which helped steady her composure. When she had recovered, she returned upstairs to finish clearing out her parents' belongings.

Kate sat down on the bed and admired her favourite photograph, a head-and-shoulder portrait of her mother, a faint smile across her mouth, her light brown hair waved softly away from her face. Kate traced her fingers over the image and tears built in her eyes.

'Oh, Mum,' she sighed. 'How on earth did a gentle lady like you fall in love with a hard man like Dad?'

Morton Reed hadn't always been so intractable and unloving. Her mother had constantly excused his gruffness as a legacy of his front-line action in the Second World War. At first, Kate recalled, when she and Pete were small, their family had been happy but, with each passing year, their father had retreated into a reclusive shell. He never smiled, and became a hard and frightening stranger. Less forgiving than her mother, and remembering her father's nightmare violent rages, Kate sighed.

By midday, she had half-finished emptying drawers and cupboards. Pete appeared briefly for a sandwich lunch before returning outdoors. Because he looked hot and pensive, Kate didn't mention Mark's visit. Pete had enough on his mind at the moment, overseeing Darnleigh's uncertain future.

By evening, Kate had finished packing away her mother's things. Downstairs in the kitchen as she prepared dinner, she watched the scorching sun fire the western sky with orange. To her surprise, Pete arrived back earlier than usual and her spirits lifted.

She cracked open an ice-cold can of beer and left it on the table for him. His boots thumped on the back veranda as he removed them.

'Dinner won't be long,' she called as he entered.

Domesticity was low on Kate's list of skills but she'd never starved and a salad wasn't above her capabilities. She preferred a camera in her hand rather than a kitchen knife and the wide open spaces of the Australian bush to the confining indoors. Pete lifted the beer in a toast and sculled it down.

'Don't fuss, Sis,' he told her as he crossed the room. 'I'm going out.'

She heard him take the stairs two at a time and, when he reappeared fifteen minutes later, he looked remarkably fresh and smart in lightweight dark trousers and a casual white open-necked shirt.

'Third night this week. You're becoming quite the socialite,' she said.

Never big with words, Pete gave a dismissive shrug and grinned.

'Be all right on your own?'

'I'm getting used to it,' she quipped. 'Make sure you eat.'

'I'll grab a meal at the pub.'

This didn't tell her a thing.

'Given our decision any thought?' he asked hesitantly.

Kate knew he meant about the sale of their home.

'Some.'

'Good. I don't want to push you, Sis, but we have to decide. I'd prefer a quiet, private sale rather than go to auction.'

He placed a reassuring hand on her arm. Concerned for Pete's future, an auction was exactly what Kate didn't want.

'I know.'

He kissed her on the cheek and she caught a waft of aftershave.

'I won't be late,' he said.

'Don't rush home on my account.'

The humour drew a grin from her brother as he left. He drove into town rather often of an evening lately, secretive about his purpose and Kate guessed there was a special woman in her big brother's life. She smiled as she watched him drive away but also felt a stab of envy. It was her own choice to have a career over marriage. Having watched her parents' relationship degenerate, she had remained wary of serious involvement.

She filled her plate with cold chicken and salad, feeling more lonely than she would ever admit, and padded barefoot into the lounge to watch the television news. Bored with the programmes that followed, she switched it off and went upstairs to wallow in a bath, letting the day's tensions ebb from her limbs. Her thoughts strayed to Mark and her inescapable future meeting with him. She knew she would be forced to explain her hatred and justify her blame when she didn't fully understand it herself.

After her bath, Kate read for a while but couldn't concentrate in the heat, thinking of Darnleigh's dilemma, Mark's offer for it, and her own personal problem with him. Even lying between cool sheets didn't alleviate her concerns and she turned restlessly for hours in the moon-washed dimness.

Eventually, she settled and woke early next morning to the beginnings of another hot day. Standing at her first-floor window to catch the light breeze before it turned warm, she revelled in the clear morning light that cast a sharpness over everything and promised perfect photography. The outdoor beckoned. Packing up could wait. She pulled on denim shorts and a sleeveless tank top. A pair of thick socks and sturdy hiking boots protected her feet. Stimulated and refreshed by a cold wash, she ran a brush hastily through her long hair and tied it back. Gathering up her camera bag, she descended the stairs two at a time for a quick breakfast.

Pete hadn't risen yet, so she squeezed enough orange juice for them both, left one in the refrigerator and drank the other. She crunched her way through a large bowl of cereal, filled two large containers with iced water and tugged on her favourite baseball cap. She stowed her gear in her small fourwheel drive and headed for the property gate where she stopped to check their roadside mail box. Uncertain how long she'd be away from the city, she'd arranged for her Melbourne mail to be forwarded up here. She shuffled through the envelopes. Still no letter about the overseas job.

With a heavy sigh, Kate climbed back into her vehicle, tossed the mail on to the dashboard and drove toward the Tree Paddock, an uncleared area of Darnleigh once used for grazing sheep, now yielding mushrooms in autumn, and flora and fauna all year.

She parked by the roadside, slung her camera bag and water containers over her shoulders, and squeezed carefully through the wire boundary fence. A short walk brought her to the shelter of the first eucalypts. She stood for a moment, absorbing the peaceful bush, comparing it to noisy city life. Part of her longed for a change of pace and the luxury of indulging her passion to capture nature through her lens but for the moment, her dream must wait. Irrationally, she almost hoped she didn't get the Paris job. As wonderful as the opportunity promised to be, the idea of travelling across Europe, lugging a carry-all and living in a procession of mediocre hotels on assignment, held less appeal than it once did. But Pete needed as much as she could earn and, quite simply, Europe meant more money.

She unpacked her gear, set up her camera and was soon caught up in another world of pursuing the perfect shot and background lighting. She loved capturing the shapes of and summer colours of the Australian bush, a curve of peeling bark, a silhouette against the sky.

Her shutter clicked until she finished one film and loaded another. As the sun climbed higher, Kate took a short break, squatting on her heels in the sparse shade of a gum tree and took a long, welcome drink.

She capped and stowed her drink container in her backpack and was enjoying a limbering stretch when the snap of twigs nearby whirled her about. She'd hoped for an inquisitive kangaroo or emu. Instead, her startled gaze caught sight of a familiar figure stiffly striding toward her through the trees. Her heart pounded wildly. What on earth was he doing here?

Judging by Mark's scowl, even visible beneath the shade of his broad bush hat, Kate feared bad news and immediately thought of Pete.

'Mark — '

'Are you all right?' he interrupted sharply.

Taken aback by his abruptness and slighted that he considered her incapable out here in familiar surroundings on home ground, she snapped, 'Of course. Why wouldn't I be?'

'Are you sure?'

What kind of question was that? They had both grown up in the bush together. His sudden appearance and odd concern were puzzling. She planted her hands on her hips and frowned.

'I'm a country girl. I can take care of myself. You doubted that?'

'Well . . . '

'You did!' she accused.

'No.'

'Then what's the matter?'

Kate found it fascinating to witness

such a big man overcome with embarrassment. Not knowing where to look, he avoided her eyes. He really had come charging out here worried about her! She was filled with relief that his neighbourly duty overrode the bombshell she had dropped on him yesterday.

'As you can see, I'm fine. I'm only photographing the bush,' she said.

'I should have known you'd be out with your camera.'

His tone was cynical.

'You make it sound like a crime.'

'I don't. I know it's your life.'

He gestured toward the road.

'That four-wheel drive belong to you?'

Kate suddenly realised Mark hadn't seen her vehicle. It had been garaged when he'd called yesterday and they had used Pete's car for the funeral. Still smarting from his slur about her photography, she glanced about and spoke with a hint of sarcasm.

'Do you see anybody else out here?'

'It could have been strangers, lost.

It's been parked there for hours.'

He must have been out checking his property to have noticed.

'Do you always go off alone?' he went on.

Kate shrugged.

'A good shot doesn't wait until you're ready.'

'You don't work in a team?'

'Not necessarily.'

'Sounds risky.'

'I prefer to be independent and call my own shots.'

She gathered up her camera again, hoping he'd take the hint and leave. She was wasting precious photography time. She fiddled idly with her lens settings so she didn't have to look at him. He paused.

'Still like your job?'

'It's a living. This is pleasure.'

A natural humility stopped her mentioning the imminent overseas promotion. Mark stepped back into the deeper shade of a bull oak and leaned a shoulder against its furrowed bark trunk.

'Pete told me you'd an exhibition of your work. Said you sold all of it.'

'That's right.'

'You're doing well.'

He sounded as if he begrudged her success.

'That an observation or a compliment?'

'Both.'

She let her gaze settle on him for a moment before responding.

'Yes, I am. I've seen pretty much all of Australia.'

No need to mention she was growing tired of it all and sought change. Whenever Kate was on assignment with a film crew and they finished work for the day, she broke free. While her workmates relaxed and socialised, Kate disappeared with her camera for hours, like this morning. She loved this country, its vastness, its contrasting scenery.

'You've established a fine career,' he went on, interrupting her thoughts.

'I've worked hard for it.'

In truth, she'd buried herself in work to escape the gremlins of the past. But, especially since returning home, they had returned to haunt her and she discovered she was not free at all.

Mark removed his hat and wiped sweat from his brow. At his gesture, Kate instinctively set down her camera, retrieved the water flask from her backpack and offered it to him. His big hand brushed hers as he accepted it. She sat down on a nearby log and waited while he quenched his thirst. When he finished, he wiped the back of his hand over his mouth.

'Thanks,' he drawled with a slow smile and handed it back.

Kate replaced the flask in her bag and straightened to find Mark standing, feet apart, arms folded, studying her. She wished he would leave but was niggled by an uncomfortable premonition.

'What next?' he asked.

Kate lost his meaning.

'I'm sorry?'

'After Darnleigh.'

'Oh. Who knows?'

For a fraction of a second, he hesitated, then moved a step closer.

'Don't shut me out, Katie.'

Oh, no! He wanted to talk. Still sensitive from yesterday's encounter, she had hoped to avoid another so soon. Feeling her old attraction for him flare up again whenever she was around him, she almost felt guilty for biting his head off the day before.

'Now?' she asked.

'It's as good a time as any.'

It would never be the right time, Kate thought miserably.

'You raised the issue, remember?' he said.

Meaning the plane crash and her accusation. She tensed, stunned by his bluntness. A thin shaft of sunlight pierced through the sparse-leafed canopy overhead and gleamed on his hair. She wanted to reach out and stroke its rich gloss, let her fingers ripple through its richness. Growing up, they'd rarely touched but when they had, Kate remembered the surge like a life force that passed from Mark's body to hers. The longing conflicted with her private animosity toward him.

'I'm not to blame, Katie.'

His words brought her back to reality and she levelled her gaze at him.

'You were at the controls when the plane went down.'

'You know the coroner's finding as well as I do.'

He tipped a finger beneath her chin. Kate felt warmed by his touch, and bleak at the same time.

'I was cleared. It was mechanical failure and there wasn't a thing I could do about it. I was lucky to get out alive myself.'

As much as she had mourned the tragedy, Mark's survival was one miracle for which she had been guiltily grateful.

'Let your emotions go, Katie, instead of holding them in to turn sour.'

'I've done no such thing.'

It was a groundless protest and they both knew it.

'And the court's decision didn't take away my hurt.'

Mark's hand dropped down and he backed away.

'What about my hurt?'

He stabbed his chest.

'Never forget, Katie, your mother wasn't the only passenger that day. I lost my father in that crash. I felt bad enough about the death of a wonderful woman and neighbour let alone my own flesh and blood.'

Mark's outburst of quietly-controlled fury startled her. Caught up in overwhelming grief at the time, she had never really stopped to consider his loss which must have been as devastating as her own. Feeling humiliated for being so thoughtless, Kate tensed when he reached out and grazed his thumb across her cheek to remove teetering teardrops from her lashes. Edging backward, she crossed her arms over her chest, her heart aching for what might have been. But Mark persisted, gripping her shoulders.

'I faced my demons, Katie. I got on with my life. You should try it.'

'I'm not like you. I can't get over things just like that.'

She snapped her fingers in his face.

'It was six years ago, and it wasn't quite that easy.'

'And now you can't wait to get your hands on Darnleigh.'

'I'm trying to help you.'

'And gobble up more land in the process,' she accused wildly.

'That's unfair.'

'Life's unfair.'

He backed off and threw up his arms in exasperation.

'For goodness' sake, Katie, what's the matter with you lately? You were always touchy but never as bad as this. At least Pete listens to reason. His future is at stake here. Forget your own self pity and think of him.'

Kate's blood boiled at the stinging rebuke.

'Pete will get every last dollar of my share of Darnleigh to set himself up on another place and I won't begrudge him a cent,' Kate said coldly. 'And what about my future?'

He stopped and cast her a quizzing gaze.

'Your future's not here.'

His statement knocked the air from Kate's chest.

'You don't think I belong here anymore?' she asked.

'Did you ever? You took the first opportunity to escape.'

It cut deep to hear Mark's allegation that she had abandoned home and family. After his wife's death, Morton Reed had shut out his children, forcing them to heal alone. At the time, blind with grief, and knowing Darnleigh would never feel like home again without her mother, Kate only knew she had to get away. For months afterwards, she had seen a psychiatrist. In time, she had overcome her grief but never resolved her blame. She had suffered alone, as they all had, so who was Mark Thornton to judge?

'You're wrong,' she said, 'but I don't give a damn what you think.'

When had lying become so easy, Kate thought sadly, pulled apart by memories and feeling immeasurably hollow in the wake of his declaration. And why should he look so bleak when he had just flung all the blame back at her and laid it squarely at her feet?

Mark glared at her, tugged his hat more firmly on his head and started to leave. After a few steps, he halted and turned back to her.

'By the way, Amelia was asking after you.'

Kate was thrown by the swing in conversation.

'Your aunt?'

'Don't ask me why,' he said, 'but she's concerned about you.'

'Tell her I'm fine.'

'That's open for debate,' he flashed, 'but you can tell her yourself when you visit. If you remember, she doesn't drive.'

Kate pursed her lips, feeling bullied as she had when they were young.

'I'd forgotten.'

'Why am I not surprised?'

His critical gaze burned over her as fiercely as the summer sun.

'She expects you tomorrow morning. And don't worry, I'll make sure I'm not around.'

3

As Mark marched away, Kate stood alone and unsure in the bush. The air had grown hot and still, and it seemed as if all the birds had stopped singing and chattering in the trees. She considered calling him back but wavered, realising the futility. She had hurt him deeply but even knowing it, she found little had changed in her mind. At the moment, their differences were too great to be resolved.

Impatiently, she swiped at her damp eyes. What was the matter with her lately? She never let herself cry. Hardened control had always worked before. When their parents had flown in the plane that day, Kate recalled her disappointment at not being allowed to go, too. If she had . . .

Louise Reed had said, 'Don't sulk, Katelyn. We'll be back soon and I'll have a surprise for you.'

That had been the last time she saw her mother, and she'd never found out about the surprise. Mark had taken away the person she loved most in her life and who had held their family together. Nothing would change that. Her mother was dead and Mark was to blame, except now she found herself questioning that tenacious conviction, long held, and perhaps unjust. She appreciated that he had suffered, too. It still confused her that she begrudged Mark his life and yet was grateful for it. Over the years, Kate had always wondered what purpose of fate had decided Mark should be the sole survivor.

Kate had lost enthusiasm in her photography, so she gathered up her gear and drove back to the homestead. Somehow, she survived the afternoon. She finished packing up her parents' belongings, locked the door to their room and resolved to leave it shut, to forget that period of her past and get on with her life.

Next day, Pete needed fencing supplies and left for town early. The air was heavy, the sky dominated by massive, thunderous cloud. It might be days or weeks before any rain fell from them at this time of year, if at all.

For her visit to Amelia, Kate chose a long, sleeveless dress in shades of ochre. With leather sandals and light make-up, she felt respectable enough to face Mark's spinster aunt. Apart from a brief hug at her father's funeral, Kate had avoided Amelia Thornton and her whispered plea to visit because she wanted to avoid Mark.

Considerate of him to stay away today, she acknowledged, as she turned her four-wheel drive on to the main road and headed for Grey Gums. Kate pulled up at the impressive, stone entrance with iron gates to the property and collected the mail from their roadside box. She noticed a coloured envelope addressed to Amelia in strong handwriting with a Melbourne post-mark. Kate tossed the mail on to the seat beside her and continued toward the homestead. She felt a nostalgic pang at her first glimpse of the station homestead for six years.

In the late summer heat, pink and red ivy geraniums scrambled unchecked over the ornate lattice work, contrasting with the grey stone walls, deep in shadow under the wide verandas. The grand, sprawling house looked out over its setting of acres of gardens; old established gum trees, ash trees and a trio cluster of weeping silver birch dotted across its extensive lawns, all hardy enough to withstand the dry inland summers.

As a girl, Kate had lived in awe of the magnificent property. Many times she had accompanied her mother to visit Amelia. Being the only females for miles around, the women had been close friends, once.

Kate chewed her lip as she pulled up on the gravelled parkway at the side entrance. As she alighted, she glimpsed a small plane standing in a paddock beyond the house. She gasped in shock. Mark still flew? She glared at the aircraft with narrowed eyes.

Suddenly Amelia appeared from the house and Kate's astonishment was diverted by their greeting. Her hostess hadn't changed a bit and Kate savoured the secure knowledge and familiarity of her unchanged appearance — the neatly-waved grey hair; the simple but expensive cotton dress and pearls. Amelia always wore pearls.

They hesitated, but only for a moment. At Amelia's warm smile, they fell into each other's arms and the years melted away. Kate's throat tightened with emotion. When they drew apart, Amelia's hazel eyes glimmered with tears. She pressed a light kiss on Kate's cheek and clutched her for a moment, then stood back to look.

'Katelyn, dear, it's so lovely to see you again. But you're much too thin.'

Kate gave an unsteady laugh.

'You always say that. And you still don't drive.'

Amelia waved a dismissive hand, firmly linked their arms and ushered her into the homestead's cool, enormous interior. Kate handed Amelia the mail.

'Oh, thank you, dear.'

The older woman blushed at the sight of the coloured envelope and tucked it into her dress pocket, setting the rest on the huge, oak dresser in the hall. Kate thought her reaction intriguing, but didn't comment as they moved into the drawing-room.

'I'm sorry, Katelyn.' Amelia frowned. 'Mark was here a short while ago but he left suddenly. I can't imagine why. It was quite rude of him. He knew you were coming. He can't have forgotten your visit.'

'I'm sure he's busy,' Kate said, trying to sound normal.

Amelia motioned to her guest, and as she sank into a deep, comfortable sofa, Kate wistfully absorbed the idyllic view,

Amelia's gracious company and the homestead's peace.

'You'll have so much to do and so much on your mind since Morton's death and your . . . er . . . situation at Darnleigh,' Amelia said kindly.

She sat down beside Kate who had forgotten Amelia's charming honesty and was thankful for it. But at the mention of her father, Kate felt guilty.

'I haven't been able to cry for him, Amelia, at the funeral, or since,' she confided. 'My heart feels like a cold, hard place with no feeling.'

Amelia reached out and patted Kate's hand.

'Morton was an unusual man. You'll grieve in your own way. Perhaps it will be more like regret. We have so much to talk about,' the older woman went on, tactfully changing the subject. 'I know it's hot, but it's cool in the house so I'll make us a pot of tea. I'm sure no-one's spoiled you since you've been home, and you haven't seen Grey Gums for years. Wander around. You'll find it hasn't changed.'

'I'm glad. So many things have lately,' Kate said wistfully.

Amelia cast her a puzzled glance as she left the room.

Kate pushed herself from the deep sofa and strolled around the room. It wasn't just the solid, old furniture that made this house comfortable. Even though huge and rambling, the homestead had always felt like a home, Mark's home, the place where he had grown up without a mother. Charles Thornton had never remarried after Ellen Thornton died in childbirth bearing their only child and heir. Amelia had become nanny and housekeeper, forsaking her life in Melbourne for her brother and his baby son.

Amelia soon bustled in with a tray of beautiful china, homemade biscuits and finger slices of fruitcake. Kate chuckled as she resumed her seat.

'What a treat. There's no fancy cooking at Darnleigh while I'm in charge.'

'Well, enjoy it while you're here.' Amelia smiled. 'If Pete is anything like Mark, he'll eat whatever's put in front of him. Besides, men don't seem to mind scratching up a meal for themselves these days, do they? Mark's perfectly competent in the kitchen.'

Kate was amazed to hear it.

'You're great for morale, Amelia. I've been feeling so inadequate lately.'

'It must be traumatic for you and Pete to consider selling Darnleigh,' Amelia said as she served the cake. 'Mark mentioned he made an offer. How do you feel about that, dear?'

'Awkward.'

'I warned him you might feel that way. I do hope he was tactful.'

Fortunately, Amelia's head was bent as she poured tea so she didn't witness Kate's discomfort.

'Pete and I haven't reached a decision yet. I don't want to sell but I know we must. I seem to have this thing about letting go.'

'No rush.'

Amelia handed her a cup and saucer.

'And believe me, I speak from a lifetime's experience. Everything has its time. Darnleigh's fate will present itself, you'll see.'

'I wish I had your confidence,' Kate said ruefully. 'Right now, Pete's future looks so unsettled. We argued constantly when I first came back. At least in the past few days we've reached a kind of unspoken truce.'

They chatted on for over an hour, Amelia relating local happenings, bringing Kate up to date about people she knew, and enquiring about the younger woman's life and work in Melbourne. When Amelia refilled their cups for a third time, Kate said, 'Enough about me, Amelia. What about you? You're looking well.'

A quick flush rose to the older woman's cheeks. She dropped eye contact for a moment but when she looked up again, her hazel eyes shone.

'Katelyn, I've never been happier.'

'Any particular reason?' Kate asked

guardedly, sipping her tea.

Amelia's hand covered her dress pocket where she had placed her letter on Kate's arrival.

'You know that I lived in the city before I returned to Grey Gums many years ago?'

'Yes.'

'Did your mother ever mention the circumstances?'

Kate shook her head slowly.

'Just that you gave up a career as a concert pianist. She kept cuttings of your performances all over the world. Mum was so proud of you.'

Amelia set her cup down and folded her hands in her lap.

'It was the most difficult decision I'd ever had to make. I knew my life would be completely altered if I returned here. In my younger days, I was an exception. Back then, women stayed at home. I felt privileged that I'd had some years to spread my wings. The pull of obligation to return to my family was much greater than my need for stardom.'

'Would you make the same decision again?'

'Probably,' Amelia confessed on a sigh. 'Times change but family love and loyalties don't. I had ten glorious years. I adored the accolades, being the centre of attention, but I wasn't a social butterfly at heart. I only endured it because I loved my music so much. But I didn't only give up my career to come back and live here. I also gave up the man I loved.'

'Oh, Amelia,' Kate breathed and sat forward in her seat. 'I didn't know.'

'No-one did, except your mother and Charles. Louise knew all about the sadness of lost love.'

Kate presumed she meant her parents' unhappy marriage.

'And now William Shelton, the man I loved — still love — has contacted me and we've been corresponding this past year. He married, eventually, after I left, and had daughters. But his wife died last year.'

Amelia's eyes sparkled.

'After thirty years, he still cares. I don't deserve his affection. I let him down badly and hurt him so much.'

Kate felt moved by Amelia's account of her rediscovered love.

'Do you still love him?'

'Absolutely. It's so hard to leave the man you love, Katelyn, but it's going to be even harder to face him again. The first time anyway.'

'You're going to meet him?'

Amelia nodded.

'The letter you brought this morning, I couldn't wait. I read it in the kitchen. William wants me to go to Melbourne as soon as he can arrange a suitable weekend. I hope it's soon. I'm terrified and excited at the same time. I know it won't be like before but I'm so looking forward to it.'

'It certainly sounds promising. I'm sure everything will work out for you.'

'Time and fate will decide that.'

Kate checked her watch, edgy that Mark might return before she left.

'I really should go.'

She stood up.

'Must you?'

'I'll call in again before I return to Melbourne.'

Amelia reluctantly followed as they wandered back down the hall.

'Of course, you'll have things to do. Oh, before you dash off, we have a glut of peaches. You must take some for Pete.'

'I wouldn't know what to do with them,' Kate admitted.

'Stew them or make jam. I have a recipe that never fails.'

'It will if I make it,' Kate muttered.

'I'll write it out for you.'

Amelia disappeared, leaving Kate resigned to another ten minutes in the house and impatient to leave. She paced the room then her heart stopped in alarm when she heard Amelia's distant voice from the kitchen.

'Mark, where have you been? Katelyn's here.'

She closed her eyes and took a deep breath. If she'd left when she planned, she would have avoided him. When she re-opened her eyes, he stood in the doorway.

'You were supposed to stay away,' she hissed.

'I gave you two hours. I'm starving. It's lunch time.'

She cast a quick glance toward the kitchen.

'I wanted to leave.'

'Well, you can't now. Amelia expects us to have a cold drink and a nice neighbourly chat out on the veranda.'

Kate groaned.

'I already have a stomach full of tea.'

'For once in your life, Katelyn Reed,' Mark whispered, leaning closer, 'don't argue.'

She tossed him an icy glare but before she could protest, Mark's hand gripped her firmly around the waist and he steered her across the sitting-room and outside. They sat down in cane chairs and eyed each other warily over a pot plant in the centre of the small table between them.

There was also no law that said she must make polite, meaningless conversation, so she remained silent. For a while, she turned away. Then curiosity got the better of her and she stole a sideways glance. He hadn't moved. His profile was almost perfect.

Mark Thornton was a true outdoors man. He and his land were part of each other. Country life did that to you, Kate conceded. It drifted into your soul, possesssed you, relaxed you, even with Mark seated opposite.

She convinced herself that she didn't care if Mark thought her misplaced out here. Despite years in the city, country blood still flowed strongly in her veins. No-one could take that away from her.

'What!'

Kate jumped at the sound of Mark's voice.

'Sorry?'

'You were staring at me. Why?'

Kate hadn't realised. Searching for an excuse, her gaze settled on the pipe protruding from his shirt pocket.

'I didn't know you smoked.'

'I don't.'

'Then what's with the pipe?'

'Reassurance.'

'Big Mark Thornton of Grey Gums. I find that hard to believe.'

His dark gaze hovered over her.

'But then you find many things hard to believe, Katie, don't you?'

Touché, she thought. She'd walked right into that one. Amazingly, it didn't grate quite so much now when he said her name that way, softly and personally. If she clenched her teeth and counted to ten, she could bear it.

Amelia reappeared soon after, bearing a tray of iced, homemade lemonade and yet more biscuits. Kate welcomed her presence. It relieved the strain of being alone with Mark. She bustled off again and returned with a bucket of peaches, a slip of paper tucked in among the fruit on top.

'Don't forget these when you go,' she said to Kate.

They had just sipped their drinks

when the telephone rang. Amelia shot to her feet.

'I'll get it. You two chat. Isn't it fortunate Mark came back?'

She trotted indoors, and Kate groaned silently. Amelia's chatty voice drifted to them from indoors. It sounded like she was going to talk for ages. Mark removed the pipe from his pocket and turned it over in his hands.

'I used to smoke, you know.'

Kate had certainly never seen him.

'When?'

'After the plane crash. Did you know that deep inhaling of nicotine supplies the false impression of soothing the nerves?'

Stunned into a deep pity and sadness, Kate shook her head.

'I even prayed for lung cancer.'

Kate's mind reeled in horror at his words but she remained silent.

'When that didn't work,' Mark continued, 'I tried to see how many beers I could knock back in one sitting before I passed out. Amazing how distorted the road becomes when you're blind drunk.'

His mouth edged into half a grin.

'I always wondered why Ted Duncan pulled me up but never booked me. I guess he decided to let me handle things my own way.'

Kate stilled, suddenly feeling sick as the depth of Mark's pain finally sank into her thick brain. Despite the heat, a cold chill seeped into her bones. She had no idea. But how could she? She hadn't lived here to witness the consequences. What could she say? Kate grew suddenly aware of the huge gaps in her knowledge about him and how, shy of all the facts, maybe she had misjudged him. The cutting knowledge alarmed her.

'You weren't alone with demons, Katie.'

His deep voice drifted over her subconscious.

'I slayed plenty of dragons for three years. Anger is fine. Grief is fine. You have to get it out of your system, not bottle it inside. Life goes on, Katie,' he said softly. 'It can stink, but it goes on. And nobody in this life is perfect.'

Kate understood his meaning. That had been her problem, believing her teenage idol invincible. After all these years, without all the facts, Kate suffered a niggle of doubt. Had she been completely wrong? She hadn't witnessed anyone else's pain. She only knew she'd struggled on desperately alone. She stood up and half-turned to him.

'It seems it was a difficult time, for all of us.'

She gripped her hands together to control their shaking. Mark rose and eyed her candidly. Perhaps to lessen her strong reaction to his revelation, he changed the subject.

'Thought any more about selling?' he said.

With forced courage, she held his gaze, softer than expected.

'I realise selling is inevitable,' she said in a shaky voice.

'Make sure you choose the right buyer. My offer's the best you'll get. You know you can trust me.'

Ironically, there lay the core of Kate's problem with him. She straightened and said with desperate appeal, 'If I couldn't trust you with my mother's life, how can I trust you again?'

Instantly, Mark moved around the table and curled his large hands around her arms, pulling her toward him, compassion in his eyes.

'That's what all this comes down to, Katie, isn't it?' he muttered, helpless agony in his voice. 'Forgiving, trusting, moving on.'

He was asking her to do all those things but she wasn't ready yet. In the light of everything he had just revealed, she needed more time to think. Then with a tenderness that bordered on unfair persuasion, Mark pressed a kiss into her hair. Kate closed her eyes and savoured it as he held her.

Kate's mind screamed to resist but she succumbed to being settled against him, wondering how she could hate a man with such a stirring touch. All sense of love and hate, right and wrong, all subsided while he held her. She longed to stay exactly where she stood but pushed herself away.

'I have to go.'

Amelia's faint laughter drifted out to them.

'Tell your aunt, thanks, and good luck.'

Mark scowled.

'Good luck?'

'She'll know what I mean.'

If Amelia's friendship with William came to anything, and she returned to Melbourne to live after all these years, Mark would be alone on Grey Gums. Her heart went out to him and the future that was changing for all of them. Mark carried the bucket of peaches for Kate as they walked along the veranda. As they stepped down into the sun to her vehicle, he spoke.

'Can't we be friends again, Katie?'

Her heart tumbled over in panic.

'I'm not sure.'

'You still blame me, don't you?'

'I have a lot of thinking to do. Thanks for explaining.'

'A problem shared.'

Another subtle hint to chip away at her resistance! In polite silence, he put the fruit on the back seat and opened the driver's door for her. Then, without any warning, he pulled her close and kissed her fully on the lips. Kate felt the sparks again that he always ignited, only this time it was like a lightning flash right through her body. When he stopped, she raised an unsteady hand to her hot cheeks. Mark eyed her with lazy intent.

Shaking, Kate clambered up into her vehicle.

'See you around,' he said, his voice warm as he closed her door.

4

Kate was still trembling as she sped along the dusty road away from Grey Gums toward home. Mark's kiss could have been a ploy, a tempting morsel of persuasion but it had certainly felt real enough and had plenty of meaning for her. Oh, it was all becoming so complicated.

She wanted love and comfort and healing, someone to reassure her that, finally, everything would be all right. Deep down, she was beginning to believe that it would. This passage of restoration was taking too long. It couldn't go on. She wanted it to end, for peace of mind but mostly to try and restore the shattered pieces of her friendship with Mark.

On her part, at least, the old attraction for him was still there, but much stronger. Mark didn't seem to want anything more than just her forgiveness and friendship. She wanted to trust him again, and that much, soon, she felt able to offer. Regardless of all the other things that came between them in their lives at present, she respected him. He had overcome guilt and grief, got back in a plane and flown again. It was hard not to admire a person with such strength.

When Kate reached Darnleigh, she found Pete had already eaten lunch and left a hastily-scrawled note that he was fencing again in the far south paddock. She whipped up a fruit shake in the blender. She wasn't hungry.

Later, she stewed some of Amelia's peaches but forgot them while she checked her camera equipment and they boiled over, leaving a burned, sticky mess on the stove! By the time she'd finished scrubbing, she was hot and restless. She prowled the house, wishing she could diffuse the tension coiled up inside her. Then a gem of an idea occurred to her and she smiled. Of course! The creek!

Reedy Creek wound slowly and lazily between Darnleigh and Grey Gums during summer, effectively separating the properties. The lethargic stream had become little more than a series of deep waterholes and would remain so until after the winter rain. It would be spring before it flowed wide and swift again. Kate savoured the filtered sunlight as it beamed down through the sparse tree tops.

She soon lay on her back, sunbathing on the large, flat rock at one end of the largest creek and their favourite haunt all those summers ago. The stone had been their diving board as kids, the sheltered swimming hole edged by sand and banks of reeds.

Kate rolled over on to her stomach on her towel. She squinted toward the low, bush-covered hills known as the Back Ranges in the west, sloping down to join one side of the vast Grey Gums boundary. She knew there were magnificent views there but you had to cross Mark's property to get there and she couldn't bring herself to ask, out of neighbourly courtesy, if he would mind. He wouldn't, but that wasn't the point. It was having to ask.

So she sighed and closed her eyes. The heat sent her dozing but not so deeply that she didn't become aware of the sound of an approaching vehicle. She sat up, pushed on her sunglasses and shaded her eyes with her hand. She saw a familiar Range Rover pull up alongside her own four-wheel drive. She cursed as Mark alighted, towel in hand.

Couldn't she ever escape him? She wondered how often he came here. Kate watched as he dropped his towel and leaned against the bull bar on the front of his vehicle as he undressed down to black swimming trunks. He waded into the deep, sandy-bottomed waterhole and, in a curved porpoise dive, disappeared beneath its cool, dark surface. Kate lay down again. He hadn't acknowledged her yet but she didn't want to be caught staring. She heard splashing and imagined Mark's powerful body ploughing through the water. He was an excellent swimmer, she recalled.

The water disturbance grew louder and closer, until she heard him heave himself up on to the rock beside her. She flinched when a shower of water droplets shocked her hot skin. Kate propped herself up on her elbows.

'Find your own rock. This one's mine,' she said grumpily.

Mark loomed over her, his shadow falling across her body. He brushed the excess water from his legs and arms, then spread his fingers in a raked path through his wet hair and chuckled.

'Now, now, Katie. Be nice. There isn't another rock and you know it.'

'Then go lay down on the sand.'

'Ah, but the view's so much better up here.'

He smiled, dropped down beside her and lay back, folding his arms casually beneath his wavy hair, beaded with moisture. Closer, Kate noticed the scar on his left leg, a long, jagged line of disfigurement extending from his thigh to just below his knee. Mark caught her stare.

'I think of it as my trophy, winning life over death.'

'Looks nasty.'

'It was at the time. It took over a year and three operations.'

Mark rubbed his hand along the wound.

'This is the best the surgeons could do. I was lucky.'

The space between them was only inches. So much bare skin, if she dared to touch it, which she longed to do.

'You've grown so beautiful in the past six years, Katie,' he said softly.

She turned her gaze up to him in mute, wide-eyed surprise. This new, flirting Mark was an enigma and she wasn't sure how to respond. She prayed the reason for his sudden interest wasn't just to get Darnleigh.

'I don't believe it. You're making a pass at me,' she challenged.

'We're both adults.'

'Yes, but we're old friends.'

'You're very attractive.'

'We're neighbours.'

'We could be more.'

His admission stunned her. Could they? Whom was she kidding? If any attraction was mutual, of course they could. Mark attracted her like a magnetic field but, as a teenager, she'd barely been noticed by him and she questioned whether he was just using her now to his own advantage, yet found it difficult to believe that of him.

She realised now that her attraction to Mark had merely been masked beneath her enmity for him. The more he penetrated her defences, the more those feelings returned.

'Disregarding the plane crash, don't lie and tell me you're not even a little attracted,' he said.

'You're rich and good-looking and

single. What woman wouldn't?' she quipped back.

'I'm not talking about other women.'

'You never paid me much attention before.'

'My mistake, but you seemed so young back then, Katie. There's an old saying,' he drawled, trailing his finger down her bare arm. 'Make love not war. Interesting thought, isn't it?'

Kate edged away from him.

'Under the present circumstances, that's debatable.'

'Meaning?'

Kate sat up and spoke with her back to him.

'You want Darnleigh and suddenly you're interested in me.'

Mark straightened beside her and looked out over the creek.

'You really know how to hurt a guy, Katie.'

When she didn't reply, he placed a hand behind her neck and gently urged her to face him.

'When you can let the past die, Katie,

we'll take this up again.'

The forefinger of his other hand traced a soft path around her mouth then his head lowered to hers for a kiss. At first touch, every inch of Kate's body burned and the sensation was a torment.

When the kiss ended, Kate asked, 'Why do you keep teasing me?'

'Is that what you think? I was thinking along more serious lines.'

'It seems we're always at cross purposes. I don't believe we should complicate matters more than they already are.'

'You're backing off again, running away.'

'I am not!'

'Don't lie, Katie. Know what I think? I think you're terrified of being swept away into the rest of your life, afraid of what you might discover.'

Kate leaped to her feet and grabbed her towel.

'You make me sound like an insecure head case.'

Mark looked up at her.

'Pete's future is settled, Katie. You know about his lady friend?'

'I guessed.'

'He has plans. He's getting on with his life. He has no problem with my offer for Darnleigh.'

Mark rose to his feet, towering over her.

'It's up to you now, Katie. The ball's in your court. But try and remember one thing. Whatever you think of me personally, on a business level I hope you're impartial enough to realise my true reason for wanting to buy Darnleigh, because I have the means to help you and Pete.'

'You mean the money,' she said bitterly, gathering up her belongings.

He cast her an exasperated look and shook his head.

'If that's what you think it comes down to.'

Kate marched away down the sloping rock with as much dignity as anyone could, lumbered with dangling cameras and trailing a towel.

'Do you still ride?' Mark called out after her.

Kate stopped and swivelled on her bare heels, shielding her eyes to look back up at him. She had forgotten he always kept horses.

'When I get the chance.'

'How about The Hundred Acres in the morning?'

That meant the great views she'd longed for earlier. She was careful to curb the eagerness in her voice.

'Why?'

'For the pleasure of your company?'

He grinned.

'Yeah, right.'

'If you don't come, you'll never know what you missed,' Mark coaxed.

She hardly needed any further prompting.

'All right,' she shrugged, injecting just the right amount of offhandedness into her voice.

'See you at sun-up.'

Holding back her delight, she turned

and walked back around the creek to her vehicle with a definite lightness in her step. Beside the prospect of filming the landscape, she discovered she was also looking forward to seeing Mark again. Through the rear-view mirror, she noticed him still poised on the rock, silhouetted against the sun as she drove away.

Kate was in the kitchen grilling two thick steaks when Pete arrived home at sunset, exhausted. With a weary smile, he headed straight upstairs. After a shower, he came back down again wearing shorts and a T-shirt, looking more relaxed. It seemed he planned on staying home for a change.

After their steak and salad, followed by Kate's rather charcoal-flavoured peaches, she began washing the dishes.

'You've had a tough day. You don't have to do these,' she objected when Pete picked up a tea towel. 'I was going to let them drain anyway.'

She'd decided it was time to discuss Darnleigh's future with Pete.

'How's the fencing going?' she asked.

'As good as I can get it with the few funds we have left.'

'You've done your best,' Kate said gently.

'Around here, that's not enough.'

'Well, don't worry about it. That won't change anything. It will all come together, you'll see.'

'That's a more relaxed attitude than you had when you first came home,' he teased.

'It all caught me by surprise. I've spoken to Mark a couple of times.'

Kate turned and caught Pete's surprise.

'Good. I'm pleased to hear it. We should talk,' he said.

'Sure.' Kate hesitated. 'Are you going to tell me her name?'

The corner of Pete's mouth dimpled and edged into a slow smile.

'Jenny, Jenny Wilkins.'

'The name sounds familiar. Any relation to Dan Wilkins who owns the general store in town?' she asked.

'Jenny is his daughter.'

'I remember her now. She was two years ahead of me at school. Didn't she train for nursing?'

Pete nodded.

'She worked in the Western District for a few years. When Martron Woodfield retired from the local bush nursing hospital two years ago, Jenny applied. We met just over a year ago when Dad had his first heart attack.'

'Serious?' Kate asked with a smile.

'She's special,' Pete said hesitantly.

Kate understood that if Pete was seriously involved with Jenny, which seemed apparent and likely, she must make it easy for them.

'We should get things settled, Kate.'

'Because of Jenny?' she asked and Pete gave an embarrassed grin.

'Probably.'

'For a guy who never gets out of jeans and a work shirt, you've been the best-dressed bachelor in the district lately,' Kate teased.

'You OK about it?'

'I'm delighted.'

'What about this place? You won't have a home to come back to.'

'Neither will you.'

'We'll find another one.'

Already Pete was speaking of himself and Jenny as a team.

'You don't have anyone in your life?' he asked.

'You know I don't have time right now. My career.'

She tried to sound convincing and enthusiastic.

'No word about the overseas job yet?'

'If I don't hear something soon, I'll phone Melbourne myself.'

'You'll get it. You're the best.'

'It's a great opportunity. Paris. But we have to sell Darnleigh first, don't we?' Kate said, forcing a smile.

'You finally agree?' Pete grinned.

'Only if we really need to.'

'We have no choice, Sis,' Pete said gently. 'At the moment, we're only paying off interest. We're not reducing the capital on our loan by a single dollar. We're just getting further into debt with no way out. A cashed-up new owner will make Darnleigh profitable again. Meanwhile, the best we can do is to cut our losses and start afresh.'

Pete sounded so hopeful and confident with no regrets about the past but she knew, down deep, he must have them.

'All right. I can see your point,' she said.

'So, we just need to consider the offers we've had from Mark and Donohue. You know whom I'd prefer.'

Kate stalled.

'Why do we need to accept one or the other? Why don't we go to auction? With the two of them bidding against each other, it will mean a higher price.'

'Prices are down, Sis. Properties aren't selling. It's a buyer's market out there at the moment. An auction would just waste everyone's time. I'd rather not put a good mate and neighbour through all that unnecessarily. We've both heard the plans Donohue has for the place. You can't want that, Sis.'

'I'm concerned about getting top money for you. The more we can get, the more you'll have to start over. You know I've pledged you my share.'

'And I appreciate it but Mark will offer a fair price. I think we should go to Mark and discuss his offer. If he buys this place, he'll take it over on a walk-in-walk-out basis. We'll only keep what we need. Grey Gums is a huge, pastoral company, Kate. Mark's managed it well. He's the ideal person to run Darnleigh.'

'Hard to imagine him owning this place.'

'We'll have our memories,' Pete said gently.

'I always thought Darnleigh never seemed like home,' Kate reflected. 'But now it comes to the break, suddenly it means more than you realise.'

Pete came over and placed a reassuring arm around her shoulders.

'It's a big change, Sis, but it's the next stage in our lives.'

'I know, but it doesn't make it any easier.'

Pete turned her around to face him.

'Hey, where's my tough kid sister?'

Kate managed a weak smile.

'Buried pretty deep at the moment.'

'How about it, Sis? Do we let Mark have Darnleigh?'

Slowly, Kate felt as if the old pieces of her life were falling away but others were coming together in their place. She hesitated.

'On one condition,' she said eventually.

'Name it.'

'That you keep everything from the house. It's the only heritage we'll have to pass down. This is all good, old furniture. It would cost a small fortune to replace it. I couldn't bear to see it sold.'

'If that's what you want and you feel so strongly about it, it's a deal.'

'I'll see Mark in the morning,' Kate said without thinking.

Pete glanced at her in surprise.

'We're only going riding,' she brushed it off.

'OK I'll tell Jen.'

Pete shared a can of beer between two glasses and they clinked them together in a toast.

'To the past,' Kate proposed.

'No,' he said. 'To the future.'

5

Next morning as Kate drove over to Grey Gums, the sun skimmed the horizon in a water colour wash of pastels. She expected great photographs from the hills.

She turned into Grey Gums and sped down the long driveway. The glimpse of Mark's plane as she drove past the homestead toward the stables still niggled at the back of her mind but Kate realised it was there because he had overcome a huge, personal obstacle. She still didn't know the reason for his invitation out here this morning but she guessed she'd soon find out.

As she pulled up, Mark led two horses out into the yard. She shrugged on her backpack and wandered over to meet him. He smiled easily and tossed her the reins of a saddled chestnut mare.

'Good morning. Remember Lady?'

Kate marvelled over the animal with delight.

'You've kept her! She was my favourite filly.'

Kate recognised the black thorough-bred Mark restrained. He and The General made a devastating team. His control over the beautiful animal was absolute.

'Ready when you are,' he said.

He boosted her up into the saddle. A light breeze kicked the hair back from her face and rippled the shirt against her body as they cantered in silence across dry, grassy paddocks toward the hills. The sun had strengthened by the time they dismounted in the foothills and tethered their horses to the straggling branches of a tree. On the uphill climb, honeyeaters, green lorikeets and other bird life darted through the bush around them.

Mark led the way but Kate lagged

behind as she stopped to film. She crouched to capture a flock of red rosellas in close-up. After a moment, she felt Mark's hand touch her wrist. She glanced up and he nodded toward a clearing beside the path ahead. A stone cairn sat back from the track. Kate moved closer to read the inscription on the plaque and saw it was a memorial to her mother, Louise, and Mark's father, Charles.

'What a wonderful thought,' Kate said, finding the gesture touching.

'They were special people,' Mark said softly.

Kate sensed he was withholding something but disregarded it. There was gentleness beneath the tough façade, a vulnerability she guessed he rarely revealed. Seeing her mother's name in print evoked a nostalgic ache inside her. When a lump rose in her throat, she broke away from Mark.

'The Hundred Acres is much thicker than I remember,' she said over her shoulder.

'I've extended it with more native seedlings.'

His deep voice came from directly behind her again and his riding boots crunched dry leaves and twigs underfoot as they hiked.

'It's certainly encouraged the birds. It's beautiful.'

She stopped for a rest and to catch a glimpse of the superb views through the trees. Mark leaned against a tree trunk nearby while she kneeled on the sandy leaf-littered ground, set her camera and filmed. After a few minutes, he tapped her on the shoulder, pointing behind, and she swivelled around for a close up of a stumpy-tailed lizard basking on a rock in the sun.

When she finished, he offered her a cold drink. Kate had brought her own but she accepted his and drank thirstily from his flask, dabbing water over her face and neck before handing it back. Mark took deep gulps then capped the container. Before they moved on, he picked a red flower from a nearby bush and, twirling it in his fingers, strolled toward her. Sunlight gleamed ginger flecks among the waves of his thick brown hair. She caught her breath as his fingers slid the bloom through a buttonhole on her shirt.

'A reward for your morning's work,' he murmured.

'Thank you.'

She smiled and thought how utterly gorgeous he was. And she'd thought so ill of him in recent years. Kate gave herself a swift, mental shake as Mark extended a hand and, for a while, she concentrated on clambering up the last steep natural steps in the rocks to the summit. At the top, she gasped.

'I'd forgotten how magnificent it is up here.'

In the distance, dams glittered in the sun like toy ponds. Endless straight roads dissected yellow and brown paddocks in rectangles and squares. Already the flat lands shimmered in a heat haze. Silence and a stiff, refreshing breeze swirled around them. Kate was filled with a profound sense of belonging. This country would always be her anchor. No matter where she travelled, Kate knew in her heart she would return here one day. She would find herself a small place and settle for good.

When one of Mark's arms casually draped around her shoulder, her first instinct was to pull away but he just stood still beside her and the moment felt companionable and right. Below them, the neat layout of the Grey Gums homestead and its surrounding home paddocks proclaimed its prosperity. Basically, Kate mused, Mark owned everything down there as far as the eye could see and, although he didn't know it yet, was about to acquire even more. Beyond the winding course of Reedy Creek and its clinging river gums, Darnleigh's rusting rooftop glinted in the sun.

'I'd look after it, you know,' Mark murmured over her thoughts.

It was time to tell him. She stepped

out of his hold and turned to him.

'Pete and I agreed to sell last night, to you.'

There was a pause while her news sank in, then he gripped her shoulders, beaming down intently into her face.

'Thank you, Katie. You won't regret your decision. I give you my solemn promise to take excellent care of it.'

Kate heaved a long, unsteady sigh. Mark looked so happy compared to her inner sadness. She still resented his profit from their misfortune but knew there had been no choice. And it was not a smile of triumph on his face, more contentment. He lifted her hand, turned it over and kissed the palm softly, a simple gesture, telling her he understood.

'Pete will contact you to finalise details,' she managed to say.

'Does this mean you trust me again?'

Kate gathered together as much confidence as she could.

'It means I believe in you, to manage Darnleigh as well as Grey Gums.'

'It's a start.'

After a pause and because it was on her mind, she said, 'You have another plane.'

'If you fall off a horse, you get back on again. Right?'

She nodded.

'Never forget, out here it also represents fast access to civilisation for safety and emergencies.'

They stood apart, no longer touching, two isolated souls on a hilltop, staring out across the vast flat world beyond, contemplating the past and the future. After a while, Mark spoke, breaking the silence.

'Katie, there's something you should know. Maybe you won't hate me quite as much. Sit down.'

He indicated the large rock behind them and she sat down.

Mark stood over her and leaned forward, one booted foot on the rock beside her. His expression looked forbidding and ominous as he began.

'First things first. Let's get this trust

thing out of the way. I need to have your assurance that you trust and believe in me unconditionally. It's important,' he added, noticing her frown.

'I've already told you it was because of the crash. Since you've explained, I see circumstances differently now.'

'Good, but we've never really got to the bottom of it, have we, Katie? Why you lost faith in me. The real reason.'

Her heart almost stopped in panic. They were moving into uncharted territory here. Eventually, she confessed.

'Perhaps.'

'Do you trust Pete?'

Kate had no idea where Mark was heading with all this.

'Without question, yes.'

'Why?'

'He's my brother.'

'What about me? Wasn't I like a brother?'

'Not really,' she was forced to admit, feeling uncomfortable.

'I thought we were at least mates.'

Kate found it difficult, embarrassing to voice the truth after all these years.

'You weren't less, Mark. You were more. You were my idol, my hero.'

His brown-eyed gaze studied her in disbelief then turned self-conscious.

'Really?'

With a wry grin, Kate nodded.

'I had the biggest crush on you. You were like a god to me. Satisfied?'

She flushed, knowing she couldn't bear it if he laughed.

'Don't you dare make fun of me!' she threatened.

'About something so important to you? Never. I wish I'd known. I'm flattered.'

'I guess I saw you through rose-coloured glasses. To me, you could do no wrong, so when I was told about the plane crash, you smashed my golden image of you into a thousand pieces and at the same time took away my mother, the most precious person in the world to me. It was like an ultimate betrayal. I guess from then on I hated you because I'd loved you yet you ruined my life and my dream.'

Kate felt vulnerable and exposed before him, and so drained from her admission she could hardly breathe. Mark cradled her face in his hand.

'I'm sorry for letting you down, even if I didn't know it. I'm only human.'

'Now you tell me,' she quipped to hide her susceptibility around him.

'You never asked,' he chided softly.

Kate shrugged.

'No reason to really.'

'Forgive me?'

It was not unknown for an apology to be above a man's pride. Mark, it seemed, had no such hesitation. Behind the strong man lay an amazingly compassionate human being. She could see that now and, at that moment, she would have forgiven him anything in the world.

'I believe I do,' she said sheepishly.

It seemed his whole body slumped with relief.

'About time.'

He straightened, paced a few steps away and turned to face her.

'Katie, did you ever wonder why your mother and my father were in my plane together six years ago?'

She nodded.

'As a matter of fact, yes, I did. It seemed odd that she didn't ask Pete and I to go with her. It sounded so exciting. I'd never flown and it would have been quite an experience. I begged Mum to take me but she refused.'

'I'm glad she did,' he said in a husky, broken voice.

A germ of suspicion gently eased itself into her mind.

'Why did Charles and Louise go up together that day, Mark?'

He exhaled a sharp breath, raked the hair back off his face in a slow, deliberate movement and searched Kate's face.

'They were going away to discuss their future together and how your mother could leave your father. They were in love, Katie, with each other.'

Stunned by Mark's announcement, Kate stared back at him.

'What!' she whispered.

'They'd cared deeply for each other for a long time and been secretly meeting for months before the accident. Dad confided in me and asked me to fly them away for a few days to make plans. Apparently, Louise had told your father she was going to Melbourne but not that Charles would be with her. A lie of omission, I guess. It may not be any consolation but their fate was how they would have wished it, Kate. They were so happy. They just wanted to be together.'

Mark pulled a wry smile.

'After twenty years of being a widower, my father finally found love again and your mother had a second chance, too.'

Kate shook her head, speechless. Louise and Charles! In retrospect, she realised, they would have been well matched. Charles was a big, strong man, roughly handsome and one of life's quiet gentlemen. Louise, charming and sensitive, would have complemented him perfectly. Finally, Kate thought with irony, her mother had found the man she deserved, but as a sheltered and isolated teenager at the time, she hadn't noticed a thing.

'Does Pete know?'

From Mark's cautious gaze, she guessed his answer before he voiced it.

'Yes.'

Appalled that her brother knew but she did not, Kate confronted him.

'Why wasn't I told?'

'You took your mother's death badly. Pete didn't want to upset you any further.'

Anger surged up through her.

'How considerate of you both to arrange my life for me,' she said bitterly. 'Finally, after all these years, everything is beginning to make sense. There are reasons and explanations for what happened. Mother was happy and planning a whole new future. Perhaps if you'd told me sooner instead of protecting me, I might have coped better. Heavens, Mark, I've felt like a mental cripple all this time. Now everything is clear.'

Annoyed at the lack of faith from Mark of which he had accused her, Kate scooped up her camera gear and began to stride away. He caught her arm.

'Katie.'

She shook him off.

'Don't worry. I believe you're telling the truth. I just don't like the way you and Pete went about it. I'd rather be alone,' Kate spat out tersely, feeling betrayed and exasperated.

Her mind buzzed with thoughts as she carelessly scrambled back down the rocks. That must have been the surprise her mother hinted at before she left that fateful day — the amazing secret about loving Charles Thornton that had been kept from her now for six years. She may have been young but she deserved to know. If Charles and

Louise had lived and married, Mark would have become her stepbrother!

Kate grazed her hands and arms as she descended too fast, aware of her stinging injuries but ignoring them. She'd always wished her mother would leave her father. Now she knew Louise had had the courage after all and Kate felt relieved and proud.

When she reached the level track again, she raced through the bush, the dry undergrowth whipping back to lash her. Back at the base of the hill, she ripped Lady's reins free, dragged herself up into the saddle and set the mare's nose for home. She heard hoof beats thundering after her. Mark didn't even trust her to have a decent gallop and let off a little steam!

Back at Grey Gums, she slid from the mare and led her into the stable. Her shaking hands fumbled with the straps. From the corner of her eye, she saw Mark leap from his horse and reach her in long, uneven strides.

'Don't ever do that again!' he

growled, breathing hard.

'Walk away from you?'

'Endanger yourself.'

'I'm not a child any more.'

'I'm well aware of that.'

His voice had turned soft and dangerous. His large hands covered and steadied hers as she struggled to unsaddle Lady.

'Leave it. I'll do it.'

Kate dropped her trembling hands to her sides.

'I'm going home.'

Mark caught her wince of pain and inspected her scratched arms.

'You're not going anywhere.'

Leading her over to a bale of hay, he commanded her to sit down. Kate relented and sank down. As Mark disappeared, Kate ran a raw hand carefully through her hair and grimaced. Incredibly, she noted with a grim smile, the flower Mark had given her had survived the ordeal intact and, although flattened, still drooped from her buttonhole. She closed her eyes and sighed. It had certainly been an interesting and eventful morning!

Her eyelids flew open at the sound of Mark's return. He carried a first aid kit and wordlessly sat down beside her, turning his attention to the damaged flesh on her hands and arms. With careful movements, he gently stroked salve over her upturned palms.

'You can stop directing your anger at me for a start. I agree Pete should have told you years ago,' he said after a few moments.

'I had a right to be told,' she snapped. 'I misinterpreted what happened six years ago because I wasn't. It's unforgivable. No-one believed in me.'

'Now you know how it feels,' Mark said quietly.

Touché, again.

'I'll tell you something. I've dodged violence and fought crowds to photograph a top story. I've kept lecherous boyfriends at bay. I've survived city life and worked hard against stiff competition to get ahead in my job. Believe me, none of those things was achieved by a weak person.'

She saw the gleam of admiration in his eyes for a moment as he finished tending her wounds then he packed up the medical kit and gave a long sigh.

'You left as a girl, Katie, and returned a woman. You've done a great job of yourself.'

Kate's brows arched in surprise at the compliment.

'Thank you. I think so, too.'

'You all right now?'

'Do you mean physically or emotionally?'

'Both.'

'I'll survive.'

'Resilient little thing, aren't you?'

His slow smile compensated for all the tension and misunderstandings between them. Fate had steered life's course for all of them six years ago. Now, with everything becoming resolved between them, they could put the past behind them where it belonged.

Staring at each other in the dimness and warmth of the stables, it was suddenly as if a light bulb had simultaneously clicked on for both of them. They each gave a silly grin. Kate felt a heady sense of awareness and attraction for Mark building up inside her. Judging by his restless gaze all over her, he felt it, too.

His hands moved up along her arms and over her shoulders until they framed her face. Just for a moment his dark eyes glimmered before his head dipped to reach her mouth.

'Katie, where have you been all my life?' he whispered between kisses.

'Here, mostly,' she breathed.

'I'm glad you came back.'

'For a little while anyway.'

She felt Mark's body grow still then he pulled away from her.

'How could I forget?'

Stunned by his sudden off-handedness, she asked, 'Do we need to?'

'Katie, you're a city girl. Your life and career are there.'

He was right, of course. In a matter of weeks, she might be half a world away, she thought dismally.

'But what about that kiss just now? Didn't you feel anything? Was it so terrible?'

He saw the desolate expression on her face and hauled her against him once more.

'Of course not. I've been looking at you for years, watching you grow, knowing you would become a classic beauty. You're a desirable woman,' he whispered, 'and I can't deny I'm not interested.'

'But?'

'I guess we got a little carried away, that's all.'

'You don't want to be adventurous and pursue it?'

He was being so casual as though the discovery and excitement that had just occurred between them had never happened or was easily forgotten.

'You'd better go home,' he replied.

'Sure, friend,' she said with a bitter twist to her words.

Mark's unreadable brown eyes roamed over her as she hesitated.

'I'll come over tonight and see how you're doing. I have an idea that might provide a solution for Darnleigh.'

'Oh,' she said, her hopes dashed.

'Tell you later.'

He leaned forward and kissed her nose.

'Scoot.'

Reluctantly, Kate dragged herself out into the midday sun, shading her eyes against the glare after the gloom of the stables. She climbed into her four-wheel drive and gunned it into life.

He wanted her but he was sending her away. Privately, she glowed. The situation wasn't entirely hopeless. She'd have to show him she was interested and determined, and make it impossible for him to resist.

6

From her upstairs bedroom window later that day, Kate watched Pete return to the homestead. In his absence, she'd had time to picture Charles and Louise together as a couple, and given her mental blessing.

She cast a nostalgic glance over the wildflower Mark had given her. It looked slightly crushed but alive in its tiny vase on her dresser and she felt dreadful for having blamed him all these years, not to mention annoyed that no-one had ever told her all the facts, but relieved that she finally knew.

She heard Pete leaping the stairs two at a time and called out to him as he passed her half-open door. She didn't mince words.

'Mark has told me about Mum and Charles Thornton today.'

Pete's shocked expression showed he

clearly understood her tone.

'It was hard, Kate, knowing how to tell you.'

'Mark managed.'

'Would it have made any difference?'

'At the time, yes. It changes everything. I've blamed people when I had no right. I've lived in a shadowy nightmare for six years thinking I had some kind of psychological problem. And all because I was never told the truth. I always sensed there was something more.'

She glared at her brother.

'Anything else you haven't told me?'

Pete's face was grim and he slanted his gaze away from her.

'No.'

'Are you sure?'

Pete flashed a defensive look back at her.

'I would have been damned if I'd told you then, and I'm damned now because I didn't.'

'It wasn't your choice to make, Pete. You took that decision from my hands, which didn't help me come to terms with Mum's death. I can tell you now, knowing the truth would have helped.'

'Maybe you should have come back home and dealt with it,' Pete said quietly.

Kate whipped around to confront him.

'Not while Dad was alive. You deserve a medal for staying.'

'I did what I thought was right at the time.'

Pete looked like a scolded pet and Kate's heart went out to him.

'I know that,' she conceded reluctantly. 'But the consequences have affected my life for so long, it will take time for me to get past my feelings of guilt and embarrassment over my stance. I'm appalled how badly I thought of Mark and how I blamed him for the plane crash. And I'm deeply hurt at being excluded from such an important issue that had such long-term repercussions on all our lives.'

'What say we share a beer and a

sandwich? My treat,' Pete suggested.

Kate was still irritated but shrugged.

'Sure. Why not?' she said, not smiling.

They headed downstairs.

In the kitchen, Kate said, 'I want you to organise the sale contract and legalities with Mark as soon as possible. He's coming over tonight. I need to get back to Melbourne and find out about this overseas job. If I don't hear tonight, I'll call them in the morning. I can only stay over the weekend, OK?'

Any longer, Kate thought, and she'd grow even more attached to Mark.

Later, Kate sat on the front veranda while Pete was under the shower and watched the sun set in a fiery western sky. The evening air was sticky and humid, filled with the background music of crickets. A change in the weather was imminent.

Soon, in the dusk, headlights appeared from the direction of Grey Gums. Mark's shadowy figure emerged from his vehicle and he stepped up on to the veranda. It was so good to see him again, even after only a few hours. He looked fresh and attractive and threatening in every sense of the word.

'Hi,' he murmured. 'How are you recovering?'

'From my wounds or your kiss?'

'Don't make it difficult, Katie,' he growled. 'What happened in the stables probably shouldn't have.'

But even in the shadows, his eyes betrayed the truth he failed to admit. A thrill of amusement zipped through her.

'Why not?'

'We should have known better.'

'Surely sometimes it's OK to let yourself go.'

With Mark, that was asking for trouble but she was up for a little excitement to lure some memories and chase away the clouds of their past. She recalled the feel of his warm body beneath her hands that morning.

'I'm not denying you're beautiful, Katie,' he said softly.

'In the dark?' she teased.

Kate heard his uneven intake of breath and sensed his hesitation.

'I can smell your perfume and I know how you feel, too.'

Encouraged by his admission, she stepped closer, deliberately brushing against him. His lips were so close. Surely he could feel her heart thudding in rhythm against his own.

'But we're only good friends, right? You're trembling and your body's as hot as mine,' she teased again.

'It's summer.'

'Nice try,' she replied, smiling wickedly.

After all these years of craving Mark, he was actually showing interest with the worst timing in the world. What sense was there in pursuing a relationship, even one she had always desired, when she wouldn't be around? In all probability, within a month, she might be living in a foreign country on the other side of the world.

Blow it, Kate sighed. She tilted up her head and kissed him. When Mark groaned and his arms tightened around her, she knew a fleeting moment's happiness. She was in danger of losing her heart. Her life was finally coming together, yet falling apart.

'Kate?'

Pete's voice and heavy footsteps came to them down the hallway.

Kate gasped. They broke apart, as though suddenly ashamed of their lapse. With unsteady hands, Kate straightened her hair while Mark did likewise. They had only a few moments to compose themselves before Pete opened the front screen door.

'Hi, mate. What's this proposition you have in mind?' he said, smiling.

'Let's go inside and talk about it,' Mark replied smoothly, stepping back and indicating they should precede him indoors.

In the old lounge, hung with a stunning chandelier and musty velvet curtains, proof of grander days, Kate served icy beer and savouries while Mark outlined his idea. Stretched out easily on the sofa, he directed a stunning question to Pete without preamble.

'How would you like to stay on at Darnleigh?'

Pete gave an ironic laugh, obviously presuming Mark was joking.

'I'd like it fine. It would save a lot of trouble.'

'I should have thought of it before,' Mark muttered. 'Pete, I won't be able to work and manage Grey Gums and Darnleigh alone.'

Kate darted him a contradictory look. He could handle ten properties single-handedly and they all knew it but she waited for further explanation.

'I have another project on the drawing-board at the moment which will take up a lot of my time.'

He glanced over at Kate seated opposite beside her brother.

'I'll need a manager for Darnleigh, Pete. Job's yours if you want it.'

Kate and Pete stared at each other in disbelief, elated yet stunned by the possibility. Mark's offer answered all their concerns. Pete could stay. He would have a job and a home and a prospect for the future. Kate's only concern was Pete's acceptance of demotion from owner to employee.

'You'd have complete freedom to run the property and autonomy in decisions,' Mark assured him. 'I know you had plans for this place. You might like to share-farm it on lease and use any capital from the sale as a deposit to buy it back. I can assure you, my terms will be more favourable than any bank.'

Beside Kate, Pete squared his shoulders in dignity and pride. Mark's proposal meant that, outwardly at least, nothing would change. Her heart opened up even more to their generous neighbour. There was no way Pete could refuse. The property sale would now become nothing more than a formality, signatures and figures on paper. Mark was effectively gifting Darnleigh back to them with the utmost dignity.

Seeing their obvious delight and interpreting it as acceptance, Mark's face edged into a slow smile. Kate hugged Pete then the two men rose and shook hands vigorously.

'Thanks, mate,' Pete said emotionally.

'My pleasure.'

Mark's smooth tone drifted warm and intoxicating across Kate's senses. She brushed what she hoped looked like a friendly kiss on Mark's cheek.

'Thank you,' she whispered.

This was a time for happiness, not tears, as she swallowed hard, straightened her back and said, smiling, 'I'll get us another drink for a toast.'

As she entered the kitchen, the telephone shrilled. Kate picked up the cordless handset on her way past to the refrigerator for champagne.

'Darnleigh.'

'Kate?'

Preoccupied in the excitement of Mark's visit and proposal, the familiar voice of her senior editor didn't immediately register.

'Paul!'

The job! She squeezed her eyes shut and crossed her fingers.

'Just tell me. Yes or no.'

'Just like that? No drum roll or anything?' he teased.

'Paul!'

The two seconds before he told her was excruciating.

'Yes.'

Kate's heart raced and then she leaned against the kitchen wall. Europe! An apartment in Paris! It was a scenario she had only ever dreamed about. A vision of Mark flashed before her eyes. If she hadn't seen him again and had her feelings rekindled, the European job might have thrilled her more.

'Kate? Are you there?' she heard in her ear.

'Yes . . . yes, Paul.'

'Congratulations.'

'Thank you,' she replied, quite overwhelmed.

'Boss wants to see you Monday,' Paul went on. 'You leave in a week.'

Seven days! Suddenly her future was rushing toward her faster than she would have liked. It felt like she had lost control over her destiny.

'I'll drive back at the weekend,' she said absently.

'I'll leave you to celebrate,' Paul's voice came down the line.

'Thanks. See you Monday.'

Her hand stayed on the receiver after she hung up. It was wonderful news, she reminded herself. It was what she had always wanted. Mark wouldn't care that she was leaving. He had put her on hold so there was nothing to keep her in Australia. Kate was gripped with a sense of finality.

She retrieved the champagne from the refrigertor. With the chilled bottle under her arm and three champagne flutes between her fingers, she returned to the lounge. Both men were deep in conversation.

'Who was it?' Pete asked, looking up.

'Paul Bennett, from the network in Melbourne.'

Pete leaped to his feet.

'You got it!'

She nodded, grinning, his enthusiasm reassuring her that it was an exciting moment after all. As she disappeared into her brother's massive hug, Kate looked over his shoulder, detecting a wariness and reservation on Mark's face.

'Good news?' he asked, standing up.

'Kate's landed a promotion in Europe.'

Pete released his sister, moved to the sideboard and began to open the champagne. The warmth in Mark's eyes turned cool. He extended a hand.

'Congratulations, Katie.'

She took his hand, enjoying its security and strength for a moment.

'Seems we have a double celebration,' he said. 'When do you leave?'

'A week.'

'You've known about this move for a while?'

'Yes.'

His gaze darkened and she instantly read his thoughts. He presumed she had just been stringing him along, all the while knowing she would leave. Kate wanted to scream he was wrong, deeply hurt that he should misinterpret the situation but unable to refute it in Pete's presence.

The cork popped, champagne flowed and her brother filled their glasses, handed them around. Gallantly, Kate thought, Mark proposed a toast.

'To Darnleigh's prosperity and Katie's career.'

Their eyes met over the tops of their glasses as they drank. The sharp bubbles cut an unpleasant path down her throat.

'With Pete still on Darnleigh,' he continued, 'you're a free agent, Katie. From all accounts, you deserve the success. How long will you be away?'

'Indefinitely,' Kate said, somehow managing to smile.

She watched him. Not a flicker of

emotion crossed his face. Kate was shot with a jolt of reality. She must have imagined Mark cared. If he did, he would have shown more feeling. Sobered by the realisation and horrified that she had virtually thrown herself at him, Kate sank into deep thought. What should have been a happy evening swiftly lost its glow.

Kate pretended interest in a conversation that centred around contracts, farming and plans. Her mind blanked until she realised there was no room for sentiment. Her career was at stake. Everything she'd struggled toward for six years was on the line. She hadn't worked hard to turn her back on a golden break into the world media scene just because of some rekindled attraction for a man who didn't seem to care where in the world she happened to be. She would be a fool to refuse the job. But deep in her heart, Kate anguished that maybe she would also be a fool to accept it.

Despite herself, her eyes focused on

the man she would leave behind. Mark caught her stare with frowning curiosity. Kate was stabbed with a wrench of grief. In that shattering instant, she realised she loved him.

'You're both invited to Grey Gums for dinner tomorrow night to celebrate,' she heard Mark say.

'Sorry, mate,' Pete apologised. 'I have a previous engagement. I'm sure Kate's free though. No reason why she can't celebrate for both of us.'

The idea of enduring polite chat over dinner with Mark spiked Kate with fear but it would be nice to see Amelia again.

'Fine. Tomorrow night.'

She found herself, in some kind of perverse form of self punishment, actually looking forward to seeing him one last time before she left.

7

Next day was overcast and sultry, the air thick with impending thunderstorms. By nightfall, Kate was edgy. Even with Amelia present, dinner at Grey Gums promised to be an ordeal.

She'd decided to wear a simple and stunning shift with side splits to the knee and shoestring straps. She'd give Mark something to remember long after she was gone. Maybe he'd even be able to scrape up a little regret.

Pete spied her when she was halfway down the stairs. Looking up at her from below, he whistled softly.

'That'll knock him out,' he said with a huge grin.

'It's a special occasion. You could still come, with Jen.'

'I have private plans.'

Kate's heart ached with happiness for her brother but disappointment for herself. Before she left, it suddenly seemed important to tell him something.

'Pete, when the time comes, whether it's with Jen or not, tell her you love her, OK?'

'I already have,' he admitted quietly.

'Then she's a lucky lady. Have a good time. I'll see you in the morning.'

Kate hugged him and swiftly strode away before her heart broke with emptiness. Thunder growled and lightning split the sky as she drove toward Grey Gums. As she neared, soft light from the homestead windows glowed out across the front garden. It was a beautiful and gracious sight and, regardless of her inner tension, Kate always felt welcome here.

To her amazement on arrival, Mark's mood had changed completely from the night before, his aloof stiffness replaced by charm and an underlying sensuality. As he escorted her down the wide hall, he ogled her snappy outfit.

'That's a racy dress you're almost wearing.'

His wicked mood excited and frightened her. As casually as her beating heart allowed, Kate shrugged off his suggestive comment.

'This is a celebration, right?'

In the sitting-room where she had shared morning tea with Amelia a few days before, the only light radiated from the soft glow of a lamp and the french windows were flung wide to receive the warm night.

Mark poured her a drink, his slow gaze travelling over her body as he handed it to her. Kate felt as though his hands were actually running over her instead of his gleaming eyes. She sipped the potent wine while he lounged against the mantelpiece, nursing his drink, amusement rife on his face at her obvious discomfort. Kate drank the rest of her wine quickly in the hope it would give her an extra dose of courage. Their conversation became an idle charade that covered the weather and the wine until Kate's nerves grew so brittle she thought they'd snap.

'Where's Amelia?' she asked nervously.

It was unlike her hostess not to come trotting in the moment guests arrived. He stiffened and cleared his throat.

'Not here.'

'Not at all?' Kate exclaimed.

'No.'

'But I thought — '

'She's in Melbourne for a few days, with William.'

Kate was delighted for Amelia. Then her heart sank with an alarming thought. That left her completely alone with Mark.

'Why didn't you tell me?' she asked, sounding tense.

'I wanted you to stay. If you knew, I wasn't sure you'd come.'

'I'm no coward.'

'Glad to hear it.'

Kate rose and crossed the room to stand at the open window.

'Amelia told you about William then?'

She sensed him move up behind her. 'Yes.'

Kate turned to him in surprise.

'You don't mind?'

'Amelia is a gracious lady who has unselfishly devoted most of her life to Grey Gums. Over the years, Dad and I told her she was under no obligation to stay but she insisted it was her home. She gave up a great deal once before. I wouldn't expect it of her again.'

'I hope it works out for them,' she said.

'Me, too.'

'You'll miss Amelia when she leaves.'

'Doesn't bother me.'

'Do you date much?' she asked suddenly, having always wondered.

Mark grinned.

'Women have floated across my path from time to time.'

Kate studied him in profile for a moment as he lounged against the door frame beside her. He must have been first in line when they handed out physical attraction. She just knew he would be an exciting lover and wonderful father. Grey Gums needed heirs and, one day, some lucky woman would bear them for him. He'd have sons, all as handsome as their father.

'You're quiet,' he murmured over her thoughts. 'Where's that vivacious woman who sauntered through my front door half an hour ago?'

'She's starving. Let's eat.'

The dining-room exuded intimacy and charm with a lace cloth and gleaming tableware, a central branch of fat candles the only light in the room. Kate was surprised and impressed. Perhaps being a bachelor didn't hurt a man after all. It had certainly forced this one to be creative.

Mark seated her at the small, round table then disappeared into the kitchen, returning with a plate of appetisers and another chilled bottle of wine. His arm rested on the back of her chair as he poured her a glass. When he filled one for himself, he sat and they ate. The tasty food stimulated Kate's appetite and the wine soothed her nerves, enough to enjoy herself.

It was too hot to hurry and their mood was relaxed. Kate helped Mark bring in the main course and they served themselves. The chicken in its tangy sauce was delicious and complemented by a glass bowl of crisp, diced salad. Their easy mood prevailed and conversation flowed, their hidden agendas shelved, old friendship revived.

Before dessert, Mark dragged his chair closer to Kate and caught one of her hands between his.

'Katie, about Darnleigh. I've been thinking. When I saw how concerned you were about selling up when I visited you that day,' he began, 'I tried to imagine losing Grey Gums under the same circumstances.'

He eyed her steadily and gently squeezed her fingers.

'It was inconceivable. I'd fight against it, Katie, just like you. What I'm saying now is that I understand how you felt and what you were going through, although I didn't appreciate it at the time.'

'You never intended to keep Darn-leigh for yourself all along, did you?'

'You and Pete are like family.'

'If Charles and Louise had married, we would be,' she observed.

A loaded silence fell between them. Kate reflected on the idea of living in the same house with Mark. Maybe it was destiny, if a tragically-twisted one, that had ultimately steered them apart.

'But you won't ever live here, will you, Katie?' he commented.

She didn't immediately interpret his meaning.

'I'm sorry?'

'Your promotion.'

'Oh. You disapprove of my career, don't you?'

'On the contrary.'

'Then what's the problem?' Kate challenged.

'There isn't one. You're an intelligent

adult, free to make your own choices. But I had you pegged as a country girl, that's all.'

'The city hasn't changed me much. Deep down I'm still the same person I used to be, apart from a few lingering hangups. And I love coming back. It will be coming up spring in Paris when I arrive,' she said with forced lightness.

Mark eyed her steadily.

'A passionate Frenchman might sweep you off your feet.'

'Not at the expense of my job, he won't,' Kate replied smartly.

'Your career's that important?'

Kate swallowed over the dryness in her throat.

'Always has been.'

Well, it always used to be — until now. Unable to bear talking about her imminent departure any more, Kate rose.

'Let's get these plates cleared.'

Personally, she would rather have left them but it gave her something to do. They piled their dirty dishes into the sink and refrigerated their left-overs then trailed back to the dining-room where they indulged in the chocolate mousse Amelia had thoughtfully prepared before she left. Afterward, replete, they lingered, finishing with a rich liqueur.

'Shall we sober up with coffee?' Kate asked, grinning.

'Maybe later. How about some fresh air first?'

As they sauntered out on to the veranda, Mark caught Kate's hand and led her down the steps into the shadowy garden. At intervals, sheet lightning lit up the inky night and the warm air pressed softly against the skin. The strong scents of jasmine and eucalyptus lingered in the air around them. He turned her to face him, slid an arm about her waist and pulled her close. His head lowered and he kissed her bare shoulder.

Her heart pounded out an erratic rhythm.

'You'd leave all this, Katie?'

His breath was warm against her neck.

'There's nothing to leave.'

Kate pushed her hands against his chest.

'Um . . . should we be doing this?'

'Probably not.'

It was as though he was teasing and testing her. So far, they had miraculously kept their attraction light and therefore safe but it could so easily become serious if they let it. If she was sensible, now was the perfect time to leave. It was not too late. There would be no harm done and no fingers burned. Should she stay and risk heartache or leave and avoid it?

Then, in the distance, the telephone rang.

Mark groaned and broke free from Kate's embrace, dashing inside to answer it. She wandered on to the cool grass. It would rain soon. After a while, she became aware that Mark's voice had stopped. She glanced back toward the homestead, rewarded with the heart-turning sight of him. She watched the powerful strength of his body as he moved toward her.

'Tom Watson from the rural fire brigade,' he explained. 'I'm on standby. Grey Gums borders the Back Ranges and they're tinder dry. I should take a look and check it out.'

'You're close to danger here. At least Darnleigh's across the creek.'

'The water holes won't stop a bushfire.'

Suddenly, conversation stopped and they stared at each other.

'I should go out and patrol,' he repeated.

Kate held her breath.

'Should you?'

Their bodies sent out waves of need to each other and tension built until it became unbearable, snapped and exploded. Mark gave in first, sighing and pulling her against him.

'I guess it can wait a while longer.'

He gave her a lazy smile, raising the tip of his finger to her lips. Kate slid her arms up around his neck. When it came, his kiss was rough and searching, as fierce as the summer lightning fizzing from sky to earth. They were losing control, Kate thought, getting carried away by the exhilarating madness of a stormy night. One of them ought to stop it.

'This isn't fair,' Mark whispered, echoing her thoughts between kisses.

Kate sighed and, in her wildest fantasy, wished he'd ask her to stay, but she had just resolved to make the most of the time they had together when she felt the first fat raindrop land on her face. Unperturbed, Mark chuckled, kissing the watery beads away from wherever they washed her bare skin. Thunder growled and lightning flashed. The downpour grew heavier and the moody night air now filled with moisture became cool and refreshing. Kate sighed, drawing away.

'I guess we should go in.'

When the rain became a stinging

torrent, Kate squealed, laughing. Holding hands they raced across the lawn to gain the shelter of the veranda. Beaded raindrops glinted in Mark's hair in the glow from the sitting-room lamp. Kate's saturated dress clung against her body like another skin. Aware of its evocative sensuality, she crossed her arms over her chest. Feeling cold now in the chilling air, Kate knew the intimate mood was lost. Mark reached out and tucked a damp strand of hair behind her ear.

'Katie — '

'I'd better go home and get out of these wet clothes.'

Witnessing her reserve, Mark cursed. 'I shouldn't have let this happen.'

'We both let it happen,' Kate said, irritated by his insinuation that she had been an unwilling accomplice. 'No harm done.'

At least none she'd ever admit, she thought, feeling confused.

Mark, on the other hand, seemed totally at ease.

'You're shivering.'

She envied his control but hated that he didn't show his feelings.

'Will you be all right?'

'Of course,' she replied, too sharply.

A swift shadow of surprise crossed his face at her terse response. Better to keep him at arm's length with false rejection than confess the truth. It wouldn't make the situation any easier but at least she'd still have her pride, Kate thought wearily.

He combed a hand through his wet hair and shrugged.

'Sure. If you say so.'

Teeming rain rattled on the iron roof, filling the strained silence between them. Mark scowled.

'When do you leave again?'

There was remoteness in his voice and eyes now. All softness was gone.

'Monday.'

'Then I guess this is bonsoir.'

Neither of them appreciated his attempt at humour and it turned sour. Looking awkward, he thrust his hands into his pockets.

Kate endured a pang of nostalgia and said, 'Same to you.'

She let her gaze linger on him a while, one last time, to burn his image into her memory, crushed by the knowledge that he didn't love her or he would admit it and beg her to stay. With her head held high, Kate walked away from him across the sitting-room toward the french doors, mustering every shred of dignity at her disposal.

The drive back to Darnleigh was a nightmare. Kate shivered with tension and refused to cry. Mark had been honest with her and she couldn't ask more than that. She must have no regrets. She had swiftly and foolishly fallen in love, and Mark hadn't. She had always loved him. Coming back home had merely flamed her old feelings back into life, she thought, as she reached Darnleigh and dragged herself upstairs.

With an ironic glance, she noticed the wildflower he had given her at The

Hundred Acres had begun to wither. Hating herself for being uselessly sentimental in the face of Mark's apathy, she took it from the vase, dried it off and pressed it between the pages of her business diary. Crushing the flower in the book felt like crushing her heart.

Kate slept badly, waking in restless fits all night. In the early hours, she awoke to a sharp crack of thunder directly overhead. She was roused by an awareness of Pete's urgent, muffled voice downstairs. She squinted at her bedside clock. Six o'clock. She scrambled from bed and went down-stairs to hear Pete's anxious voice on the two-way radio in the study. As she headed in his direction to find out what was happening, the telephone rang.

Kate grabbed it as Pete appeared in the hall wearing only jeans and a worried expression. She held her hand over the mouthpiece.

'For you. What's up?'

'Lightning started a bushfire in the

Back Ranges last night.'

Kate stared at him as he took the call, instantly understanding. The Back Ranges bordered Grey Gums. With ferocious winds, The Hundred Acres and, farther down, the homestead, would be directly in its path.

8

'What can I do?' Kate asked as she handed the phone to Pete who, like many district men, was a volunteer firefighter.

'Get dressed and answer this phone so I can get out of here.'

Kate fled upstairs. It only took her five minutes to shower and another five to dress. Despite the heat, she pulled on jeans, a T-shirt, thick socks and sneakers. A bushfire meant sensible clothes.

The district had experienced good winter rains last winter and the thick undergrowth was ideal fuel for a hungry fire. With a hot, driving wind pushing the flames through inaccessible hill country, the fire would be difficult to fight. A short while later, Kate met Pete downstairs in the hall. Frowning, she followed him to the back door where he grabbed his hat from its usual hook on the wall.

'This will be a tough one,' she said.

He laid a reassuring hand on her arm.

'Don't worry, Sis. Grey Gums is in the biggest danger but we'll be supported by helicopters and small planes. Mark's going up in his.'

Kate grew alarmed at Pete's casual piece of information. Then she stopped her rising panic, realising her fears were for Mark's safety, not his ability. Pete was halfway out the back door when a small white car pulled up outside. A young woman alighted and crossed the yard to the veranda. She was average height, barely topping Pete's shoulder, with a friendly, round face and a riot of light brown curls. Pete kissed the new arrival and Kate's heart warmed at the natural gesture.

'Hi, Jen. Thanks for coming. Am I glad you weren't on duty.'

'I'm a nurse. If I can help . . . '

'Kate, you remember Jenny Wilkins?'

They barely had time to acknowledge each other before the phone rang again. Dashing down the hall to answer it, Kate waved at Pete.

'Go. I'll take it.'

It was Mark. At the sound of his voice, a fresh invasion of emotions was unearthed within Kate. She gripped the telephone tightly.

'Kate, I need your help.'

He sounded tentative and unsure.

'Of course. We're neighbours.'

'Amelia's heard about the bushfire in Melbourne and insists on coming home. William's arranged a charter flight. Can you drive out to the aerodrome and pick her up when she arrives?'

Kate agreed. They finalised times and details, keeping their conversation brief and formal. Soon after, Pete radioed in, advising her they were setting up a fire co-ordination area in Grey Gums' home paddock, south of the homestead.

After breakfast, Kate and Jen made their first large box of sandwiches.

From the kitchen, they saw the thick smoke haze from the fire already filling the sky with a threatening pall. Jen left for the base camp with the food with the intention of remaining to help the volunteers and Kate sped in her own vehicle toward the small country aerodrome, to meet Amelia's plane. Heavy banks of smoke rose from the bush-covered ranges, darkening the morning. But what was worse, from the fire's front, huge walls of orange flame licked skyward, eating their way slowly down the hills. It was an alarming, heart-stopping sight. The rushing inferno might take days to control.

Half an hour later, Kate was back at Grey Gums homestead with Amelia.

'There's no cause for alarm at the moment,' she reassured the older woman as she set down her luggage in the hall.

Amelia patted Kate's hand.

'My future will be in Melbourne,' she said and cast Kate a knowing glance, 'but I had to come back.'

Kate smiled her understanding.

'Amelia, that's wonderful news.'

She pushed aside a rush of regret. All these people finding happiness. First Pete, now even Amelia. When would it be her turn?

Since Amelia seemed distracted, Kate boiled the kettle and they sat at the kitchen table until it was ready.

'Tell me what happened in Melbourne,' Kate urged.

Amelia pressed a hand to her flushed cheek.

'It was though time had never passed. William proposed and I accepted.' Kate gasped with amazement and hugged her.

'It all happened so quickly,' Amelia continued. 'I feel as excited as a young girl but we're both so sure. We're only having a small, simple ceremony with William's family and Mark, of course. I'd like you and Pete to be there, too, Katelyn, dear. You're like a son and daughter to me.'

Instant concern rushed into Kate's mind.

'When will it be?'

'The middle of next month,' Amelia announced hopefully.

Kate felt a keen sense of disappointment.

'Amelia, I'm so sorry. I'm leaving for Paris in a week.'

'Why, I had no idea! You didn't say a word.'

'I wasn't sure until a few days ago. I didn't like to say anything in case it didn't materialise.'

'Well, I'm sure it's a wonderful opportunity, dear, and a further step in your career. It's fortunate, isn't it, that you have no personal ties here?'

She flashed Kate a sly glance, folded her hands calmly in her lap and, in apparent innocence, proceeded to explain.

'Seeing William after all these years made me realise that if I had my time over again, I wouldn't make love wait. I would grasp it,' she said fervently.

157

Amelia's comparison was so uncomfortably close to her own situation with Mark, Kate suspected the words had been deliberately directed at her. But what could you do if your love wasn't returned or acknowledged? Feeling uneasy, Kate rose, gathering up their cups and saucers.

'Well, I'm happy for you both. Now we'd better stop chattering and get more food out to the camp,' she said.

Later, driving out to the home paddock to deliver more sandwiches, Kate was amazed at the build-up of activity. She spoke briefly to Jen but didn't linger at the base camp, where tired and dirty firefighting crews returned in teams, thankful of relief.

All day, Kate and Amelia continued preparing food for the firefighters. It was all they could do while the volunteers fought to save the bushland and station property below. From time to time, they found themselves staring out of the homestead windows in silence, watching the distant fireball shooting into the air and its wide front devouring everything in its path in a black line, drawing ever closer toward them. Pushed by a hot summer wind, it would reach The Hundred Acres first before the stubble paddocks, the last and easily-demolished obstacle before the homestead block.

The regular drone of aircraft and beating of helicopter blades were more often seen than heard, the planes not always visible through the grey curtain of smoke that settled overhead. Once, Kate caught sight of what she thought was Mark's plane as it emerged from the smoke blanket, flew low over the homestead, banked sharply then disappeared from view.

At the time, Amelia had placed a gentle hand on her arm.

'He won't take any risks. He's fighting for Grey Gums, remember?'

If anything happened to Mark up there, history would repeat itself and Kate knew she couldn't bear his loss. Although she was edgy for his welfare and concerned at the threat to Grey Gums, Kate was restless to return to Melbourne as soon as the bushfire was under control, hoping time and distance would diminish her private anguish.

Mid-afternoon, while Amelia rested, Kate cast a furrowed gaze westward and eyed the approaching fire. It was halfway down the ranges and heading for The Hundred Acres. Suddenly, it seemed important to capture the beauty of Mark's special place for him. Unless the wind dropped or changed direction, the tranquil bushland, like thousands of acres of hill country already, would soon be destroyed.

Anxious, Kate snatched up her camera gear, which she had instinctively packed when leaving Darnleigh that morning. Leaving a note for Amelia, she jumped into her four-wheel drive, heading through the scrubby bush to the foothills. Leaving her vehicle, Kate scrambled uphill lugging her camera.

She began to photograph the thickly-timbered area, planning to send the pictures to Mark when they were developed. With no time to lose, she worked quickly, blanketed by drifts of thick smoke. She recalled the morning she went riding with Mark, how secure she had felt when he held her after they reached the hilltop. Kate's eyes pricked with tears of emotion that flames would soon consume this precious bush, so important to Mark.

As always, once engrossed in her photography, Kate grew oblivious to her surroundings. She only became aware of another presence when a vehicle door slammed. Startled, she spun around. Mark's face was dark with rage, his body taut as his gigantic strides brought him to Kate.

'What on earth are you up to?' he bellowed.

'I was just — '

'I know exactly what you're doing. You're a mercenary photo-journalist making money from someone else's tragedy.'

Speechless, Kate's mouth dropped open. Knowing her, how could he accuse her of such base insensitivity? It was unforgivable.

'Getting a scoop picture pump the adrenalin, does it?' he went on.

Seething at Mark's unfounded criticism and not giving a damn what he thought of her, she snapped out, 'There are many ways I get my kicks, Mark, but exploitation isn't one of them.'

'You're putting your life in danger. Take your camera and your wheels and get out of here.'

She could see it would be useless to explain. Mark had already made up his mind about her reason for being there.

'You're wrong about me,' was all she said.

'I know an ambitious woman when I see one.'

Kate flashed him a black glare then swung herself and her camera gear into her car and slammed the door. The vehicle skidded as she roared away.

Ten minutes later, Kate stormed back into the kitchen at Grey Gums to Amelia's stare of amazement. Looking fresh after her rest, Mark's aunt remained tactfully silent. Furious and indignant, Kate folded her arms, firmed her mouth, and paced. Boy, would she give him a well-deserved piece of her mind when he got back. No, on second thought, she wouldn't waste her breath. When Kate's anger eventually subsided, she spoke to Amelia.

'Mark didn't believe I was only photographing The Hundred Acres before it was devastated. He thought I was only after a picture for the paper.'

'Don't upset yourself, dear. I'm sure he was just concerned about you. I'll make you a nice cup of tea.'

Kate remained standing to drink it, staring out of the kitchen window toward the smoke-covered hills, sickened to see the flames already licking at the perimeter of The Hundred Acres. She turned away.

In the late afternoon, it became eerily quiet. The homestead reeked of smoke and the kitchen clock ticked above the silence.

'The wind's dropped,' Kate said, frowning.

'At least it might hold up the fire,' Amelia said.

But not before it took Mark's precious flora and fauna reserve, Kate thought. When thunder rumbled overhead, they shared a hopeful glance.

'Maybe the firefighters will get lucky with a rain storm.'

The first drops of rain landed like giant stones on the homestead's iron roof. It was soon followed by the wonderful sound of a downpour, the kind that lasted for hours. Kate and Amelia smiled at each other.

In the following hours, through a haze of driving rain, they saw the first tankers gradually pull out, their exhausted crews going home for a well-earned rest. Those men who remained, Kate knew, would patrol the desolate blackened site and douse smouldering logs and stumps.

Kate sighed over the soul-destroying sight in the distance and imagined how Mark must feel. He would return soon and she must gather the courage to face him. She couldn't leave without knowing he was all right.

A short time later, Pete's utility pulled up at the homestead. Dirty and dishevelled, he dashed over the veranda and came inside.

'I'm afraid we've got some trouble,' he announced.

Kate frowned, seeds of disquiet sown by his words.

'What sort of trouble?'

'Mark's in a spot of bother. Had to make a forced landing.'

9

Kate's mind went blank but somehow she managed to ask, 'Is Mark all right?'

'Far as we know. He gave us his position before he landed. I'm going out to get him now.'

'Not without me, you're not,' Kate said.

She fetched Mark's oilskin and, pulling it on, followed her brother.

'I've already contacted Jen on the radio. She's meeting me at the south gate in the home paddock. There's only room for two in my jallopy.'

'No problem,' she replied, rattling her keys. 'I'll take my vehicle.'

Pete climbed into his vehicle and Kate followed him away from the house. He stopped to collect Jen and they continued. Before long, the outline of Mark's small plane loomed ahead of them through the rain. Kate's heart thudded. As far as she could see, the aircraft was still intact but its nose had plunged forward into the mud. There was no sign of the pilot.

Pete leaped out of his vehicle with Jen close behind, clutching a first aid bag. Kate scrambled out into the downpour after them. Deep tracks were gouged into the ground where the plane tyres had hit the soft, wet earth on landing and they ran alongside them towards the tilted aircraft. Pete vaulted up on to the wing and opened the cockpit door.

Kate held her breath. Oh, God, please let him be all right, she prayed. She craned a look over Pete's shoulder and saw Mark's familiar tousled head leaning back, his eyes closed. Suddenly they opened and he turned.

'What took you so long?'

Kate slumped against the fuselage, the rain on her face mingling with salty tears of relief.

'You OK, mate?' Pete chuckled.

'Just resting my eyes,' Mark drawled.

Pete helped him out and down on to the ground where Jen began a careful examination. Kate edged closer to see and was appalled that one side of Mark's face and forehead was cut and bleeding.

'What, no camera, Katie?' he said harshly as he spotted her.

Deeply hurt by Mark's words, Kate stepped back. He couldn't have made it plainer that she was unwelcome in his life and the knowledge stung.

'I'll go back to Grey Gums and tell Amelia he's OK,' Kate told Jen quietly.

On the return drive, Kate finally let tears of relief and anger slide down her cheeks. She wasn't crying out of self pity, she told herself, and she certainly wasn't wasting any tears on Mark. He didn't deserve them. She hoped she never saw the aggravating man again as long as she lived!

Back at Grey Gums, Kate strove to be succinct and unemotional as she related the basic details about Mark to Amelia.

'Katelyn, dear, you've had a long day. You must be exhausted. Why don't you get out of those wet clothes and take a bath?'

Kate didn't want to be around for Mark's return but by the time Pete and Jen took him into hospital for observation, it might be hours before they were back. A bath sounded like bliss.

'Sounds irresistible,' Kate agreed.

Amelia looked delighted by her decision.

'I'll bring fresh towels and rustle up a change of clothes.'

Kate wallowed at leisure in a hot, sudsy bath and it was almost an hour before she emerged from the warm, scented water. Amelia had found a black pair of Mark's track pants that had shrunk in the wash, still too big but they sufficed. His blue shirt hung to her knees but she fastened it up, rolling the sleeves up to her elbows.

As she crossed the hall, half-hidden while towelling her wet hair, she slammed straight into Mark's chest.

Kate gasped at the impact and silently moaned at the unwelcome sight of the man she least expected to see. He reached out to steady her. The dark, sombre gaze he cast over her gathered in every inch of her softly vulnerable appearance.

Jen had done a neat job of bandaging his wounds, Kate noted, but bruises were already visible on his face. His hair, although dusty from the long day's work, was appealingly tousled. Kate thought she had never seen him look more disturbingly handsome.

'Shouldn't you be in hospital?' she queried.

'No,' he replied shortly.

'In other words, you refused to go,' she said dryly.

'More or less.'

'Are you all right?'

'I'll survive.'

So official, so formal, when only last night they had almost let themselves go. The deep gaze that searched her body took her breath away.

'Blue suits you,' he murmured, scowling, as though he hated to admit it.

'Close your mouth, Mark. You're drooling.'

Kate couldn't resist a jibe and added, 'Excuse me.'

'Katie.'

She hesitated mid-step. Would he apologise? Ask her to stay?

'Thanks for helping today and staying with Amelia.'

Kate's shoulders sagged in the wake of yet another dashed hope.

'Anyone else would have done the same.'

Mark made no attempt to explain or redeem his wounding taunts. When he refused to take advantage of the opportunity, Kate decided on one last test. She would see if the great Mark Thornton was really so tough.

'Before I go,' she said, smiling.

She swaggered seductively back up to him and pressed her warm body against his. Mark's dark eyes clouded.

'What are you doing?'

'Saying goodbye.'

'Katie, don't.'

'Don't tell me a big man like you is scared of a little thing like me?'

'You have built-in weapons I can't fight,' he growled.

'Do you have to?'

'What about your Paris job?'

'I could defer.'

'No!'

'Amelia will be gone. You'll be all alone,' she teased.

'I'll manage.'

'So you keep saying. It must be such a comfort not needing anyone.'

Despite his casual attitude towards her, Kate couldn't believe he didn't feel the same as she did. Standing on tiptoe, which brought their faces closer, she plunged her fingers through his hair, ignoring any soreness he might feel, and drew his mouth down to meet hers.

Gently, she let her lips melt over his. Slowly, she felt him begin to stir and respond. Had he wanted to, Mark was

172

more than capable of breaking contact at any time but Kate noted with satisfaction that he didn't bother. But he kept his hands rigidly at his side. Finally, Kate stopped kissing him but her hands rested on his chest.

Breathing raggedly, Mark drew away. For a fleeting moment, she noticed a hunger flare in his eyes but as swiftly as it appeared, he masked it and became unreachable once more. He was tempted, but resisted. She appealed to him mutely with her eyes, but he looked away.

Oh, for goodness' sake, she screamed silently, just open your mouth and say it, you great blind oaf. It won't hurt a bit.

But she waited and it didn't come. OK, that's it, she thought. The next move was up to him. With a sigh of resignation, Kate hid the pain in her heart and walked away. She didn't look back, her misery overwhelming.

Back at Darnleigh, Pete and Jen were preparing dinner in the kitchen. Kate declined their offer to stay and join them. Although it was late, she had to leave. Calmly and sensibly, she went upstairs to pack.

Within half an hour, she had said farewell to Jen and Pete and was cruising along the Western Highway, every mile taking her farther away. She fixed her unseeing gaze on the dark road ahead. If it took the rest of her life, she would forget him. One day, she hoped Mark Thornton would regret letting her go.

10

One week later, Kate watched the city traffic flash by as the taxi drove her along the motorway to Melbourne airport. She hoped she never lived through anything like the past seven days again. They had been the most miserable of her life. Every working hour had been spent in a whirl of checking passports and visas, and becoming acquainted with details of the paper's European bureau. She had worked overtime to shorten the lonely nights, and rarely ate. How much longer would this wretched heartache continue, she wondered, as the airport came into view.

She had posted the photographs of The Hundred Acres to Mark, keeping a set of prints for herself as a kind of warped reminder of happier days, to be tormented by whenever she thought of him and regretted her mistake in leaving without a more determined fight. Amelia was right. She should have trusted her heart, forced Mark to admit his feelings and beg her to stay.

Pete and Jen had telephoned during the week with news of their engagement. She promised to return from Europe for their wedding in twelve months after their first harvest when they were more financially on their feet.

At the airport, Kate tucked her handbag and diary under her arm and waited in the queue to check in her luggage. As she placed her two heavy suitcases on the scales, she became aware of a startled look from the check-in clerk. There appeared to be some sort of disturbance behind her. Before she could turn around to investigate, strong brown hands clamped on to her suitcase and she heard a familiar and stirring masculine voice.

'I'll take these,' it said.

Her heart almost stopped and her

throat went dry when she caught sight of the man she thought she might not see again for years.

'What are you doing here?' she hissed.

'Amelia explained about The Hundred Acres,' Mark replied.

'So did I, remember? Why didn't you believe me?'

He grinned sheepishly.

'Because I'm an idiot.'

'Now you're talking,' she snapped.

'Speaking of which, we need to do a lot of it,' he growled and dragged her away from the line of people.

'I don't have time! I'm about to board a plane,' Kate choked out in exasperation even as expectancy rose inside her.

She fixed him with a murderous glare. If he was here for the reason she thought . . .

'Then you have a quick decision to make,' he went on.

Kate's annoyance intensified.

'Decision?'

'Whether you're coming with me or not.'

'I'm not going anywhere with you,' she snapped, having absolutely no intention of making it easy for him.

She struggled free of Mark's hold. Trying to handle a laden shoulder bag, a cabin bag, her diary and a handful of tickets, Kate dropped the diary. A dried red wildflower fluttered from between its opened pages and settled at their feet. Not realising what it was at first, Mark bent to pick it up.

'Yours?'

He studied the dried bloom and twirled it absently in his fingers. She watched helplessly as its significance finally dawned. His amused gaze penetrated her defenceless stare.

'A souvenir?'

Kate flushed. She snatched back the flower and replaced it in her diary. Firm fingers circled her wrist as she did so.

'You don't really want this Paris job, do you, Katie?'

Kate gazed off blindly across the

emptying departure lounge and gave a negligent shrug.

'I'm going, aren't I?'

He planted two fingers resolutely beneath her averted chin, forcing her eyes back to him. She lowered her lashes to shield her gaze, focusing somewhere around his neck. His thumb stroked her cheek.

'Look at me.'

When she did, his rich brown eyes burned with smouldering intensity.

'Truth time, beautiful. Paris or me?'

Her knees weakened at the endearment but she needed to hear three small words. No way would she lower her pride until he said them.

'I have to earn a living, Mark.'

She circled the issue, but he shook his head.

'Not good enough. Straight up.'

'I don't care if it's not the answer you want,' she hissed, suffering bypassers' stares. 'It's the answer you get.'

'I'll ask you again. Do you want to photograph news or the bush?'

She couldn't lie, not to this man, not ever. Her admission came with soft reluctance, embarrassment and a grudging lack of enthusiasm.

'The bush,' she mumbled.

Mark's mouth split into a wide, adorable grin, lighting up his entire face. Kate wanted to sink against him, give in right then. But she waited. He still had a long way to go.

'Let's get out of here,' he growled in a wicked undertone.

He still hadn't said it. Did she have to hold up a cue card with the words? He curled his fingers possessively through hers and hauled her aside. Kate trotted after him, powerless to escape his grasp.

'What do you want with me?' she demanded, frustrated.

'That's a leading question,' he replied smoothly.

'Why are you doing this?'

'Because you're difficult and you're forcing me. You're supposed to fall into my arms.'

Kate gasped with indignation.

'You're the most infuriating person I've ever met.'

Mark stopped abruptly and she slammed into him.

'Steady on, Katie,' he said, 'or I'll think you only want me for my body.'

He looked about and cursed.

'Isn't there any place private around here?'

His gaze locked on to the row of lifts. He led her inside one of them and jabbed a button. Even before the doors closed and the lift moved, he started kissing her madly. She couldn't think or concentrate on anything other than being transported above reality into another world — his world, a world she never wanted to leave. Eventually, he stopped kissing her.

'Katie, I want you so much,' he groaned. 'I need you.'

With blood thundering through her veins, chest heaving she knew she wanted the same thing but remained disappointed.

'If you came all the way just to tell me that,' she breathed raggedly, 'then you've wasted your time. You should have just telephoned.'

He cradled her face in his hands, his eyes stormy with open desire.

'What do you mean saying that? I just spilled my heart out to you.'

The lift stopped and the door opened. Mark pressed another button and turned his concentration back to Kate.

'Now it's your turn.'

'For what?'

'Don't be thick, Katie. Tell me how you feel.'

She scoffed at his audacity in expecting her to admit her love when he refused himself.

'In your dreams, Thornton.'

'You have been,' he growled. 'Constantly, erotically, which proves that I was not born to be celibate.'

'What do you want?' Kate snapped. 'An affair?'

He nodded, grinning, and a wave of

hair tumbled over his forehead.

'A lifetime affair, Katie. What we've got goes much deeper than physical desire, doesn't it?'

He knew it, too. What they had wasn't for the moment. It was for ever. As the lift slid to a halt and the door opened, a group of people waited.

'This one's occupied,' Mark told them. 'Use the next one, please.'

Before their disbelieving stares, he set the lift into motion again.

'You can't keep doing that,' Kate objected.

He caged her between his arms against the wall.

'Right now, I'm in the mood to do anything I please.'

'Are you suggesting I meekly trot off into the sunset with you?'

'Of course.'

He was so arrogant, Kate fumed. This was his last chance, his absolute last chance. If he didn't take it, she would die.

'Give me one good reason.'

'The same reason you want me.'

His voice turned husky, and this time it came.

'I love you and I can't imagine life without you.'

'Why didn't you tell me sooner?'

'I didn't want you to give up your career, like Amelia.'

Tears filled Kate's eyes, then his head came down and he kissed her with aching tenderness. Afterwards, he challenged her softly.

'If you can tell me you don't love me, I'll walk away and never interfere in your life again.'

He'd said the words she'd yearned to hear. It wasn't fair to keep him waiting any longer.

'I want you, too,' she teased, postponing the inevitable a fraction longer.

'Now we're making progress. And?'

She slithered her arms up around his neck and smiled.

'I'm madly in love with you.'

He responded to her confession with

a wide grin. The lift doors opened. The gathered crowd waited with patient amusement, realising what was happening and watching the evolving escapade.

'And?' Mark prompted again.

Kate's eyes blinked wide.

'And what?' she muttered desperately.

'And you'll marry me,' he said.

'You haven't asked.'

'If I did, what would you say?'

'Ask me and find out,' she fenced.

'Get on with it, mate. We want the lift back,' someone called out from among the spectators.

To Kate's horror and delight, Mark kneeled down before her, gathered her slender hands into his large brown ones and asked, 'Katelyn Louise Reed, will you marry me as soon as possible?'

Suddenly shy in front of the watching crowd and amazed that he remembered her full name. Kate whispered, 'Yes. Now get up.'

The observers applauded as the

oblivious couple lost themselves in a deeply-passionate kiss. When they surfaced, Mark pulled her from the lift, bowed to the applauding crowd and whisked her away. They stopped briefly to retrieve her luggage and inform the airline that she had cancelled her flight, then Mark led her toward an exit.

'Where are we going?'

Mark looked down at her and smiled. 'Home.'

To Kate, it sounded like the most beautiful word in the dictionary.

As they walked out across the Tarmac in the mildness of late afternoon, Kate's heart sang. This was where she belonged, beside this man. She barely noticed when they halted before a familiar light plane. Dark swirls of Mark's thick hair were tugged awry by a light breeze. He dropped the suitcases and squeezed her hand, pulling her against him to steal a slow kiss. Kate melted with the intoxicating softness of it.

He glanced at her. Seeing the

question in her returning gaze, he explained.

'I've had the plane repaired. There was only minor damage. Today was its test flight.'

He watched her carefully as she hesitated. For signs of distrust, she wondered, but Kate looked lovingly into the deep brown eyes of the man who would be her partner through life.

'I love you, Mark, and I trust you, completely. Take me home.'

THE END

SUMMER IN
HANOVER SQUARE

Charlotte Grey

The impoverished Margaret Lambart is suddenly flung into all the glitter of the Season in Regency London. Suspected by her godmother's nephew, the influential Marquis St. George, of being merely a common adventuress, she has, nevertheless, a brilliant success, and attracts the attentions of the young Duke of Oxford. However, when the Marquis discovers that Margaret is far from wanting a husband he finds he has to revise his estimate of her true worth.

CONFLICT OF HEARTS

Gillian Kaye

Somerset, at the end of World War I: Daniel Holley, unhappily married to an ailing wife and father of four grown-up children, is attracted to beautiful schoolteacher Harriet Bray, but he knows his love is hopeless. Daniel's only daughter, Amy, who dreams of becoming a milliner and is caught up in her love for young bank clerk John Tottle, looks on as the drama of Daniel and Harriet's fate and happiness gradually unfolds.

THE SOLDIER'S WOMAN

Freda M. Long

When Lieutenant Alain d'Albert was deserted by his girlfriend, a replacement was at hand in the shape of Christina Calvi, whose yearning for respectability through marriage did not quite coincide with her profession as a soldier's woman. Christina's obsessive love for Alain was not returned. The handsome hussar married an heiress and banished the soldier's woman from his life. But Christina was unswerving in the pursuit of her dream and Alain found his resistance weakening . . .

THE TENDER DECEPTION

Laura Rose

When Sophia Barton was taken from Curton Workhouse to be a scullery-maid at Perriman Court, her future looked bleak. Was it really an act of Providence that persuaded Lady Perriman to adopt her as her ward? Sophia was brought up together with the Perriman children, and before sailing with his regiment for India, George, the heir to the title, declared his love. But tragedy hit the family and Sophia found herself caught up in a web of mystery and intrigue.

CONVALESCENT HEART

Lynne Collins

They called Romily the Snow Queen, but once she had been all fire and passion, kindled into loving by a man's kiss and sure it would last a lifetime. She still believed it would, for her. It had lasted only a few months for the man who had stormed into her heart. After Greg, how could she trust any man again? So was it likely that surgeon Jake Conway could pierce the icy armour that the lovely ward sister had wrapped about her emotions?